LITTLE DO YOU KNOW

ADAM NIKSIC

Copyright © 2024 Adam Niksic

All rights reserved. This book or any portion thereof may not be reproduced or used in any manner whatsoever without the express written permission of the publisher except for the use of brief quotations in a book review.

Front cover and formatting by Champagne Book Design
www. Champagnebookdesign.com
Printed by Amazon Publishing
First printing, 2024.
www.adamniksic.com.au

I've never seen any life transformation that didn't begin with the person in question finally getting tired of their own bullshit.
—Elizabeth Gilbert

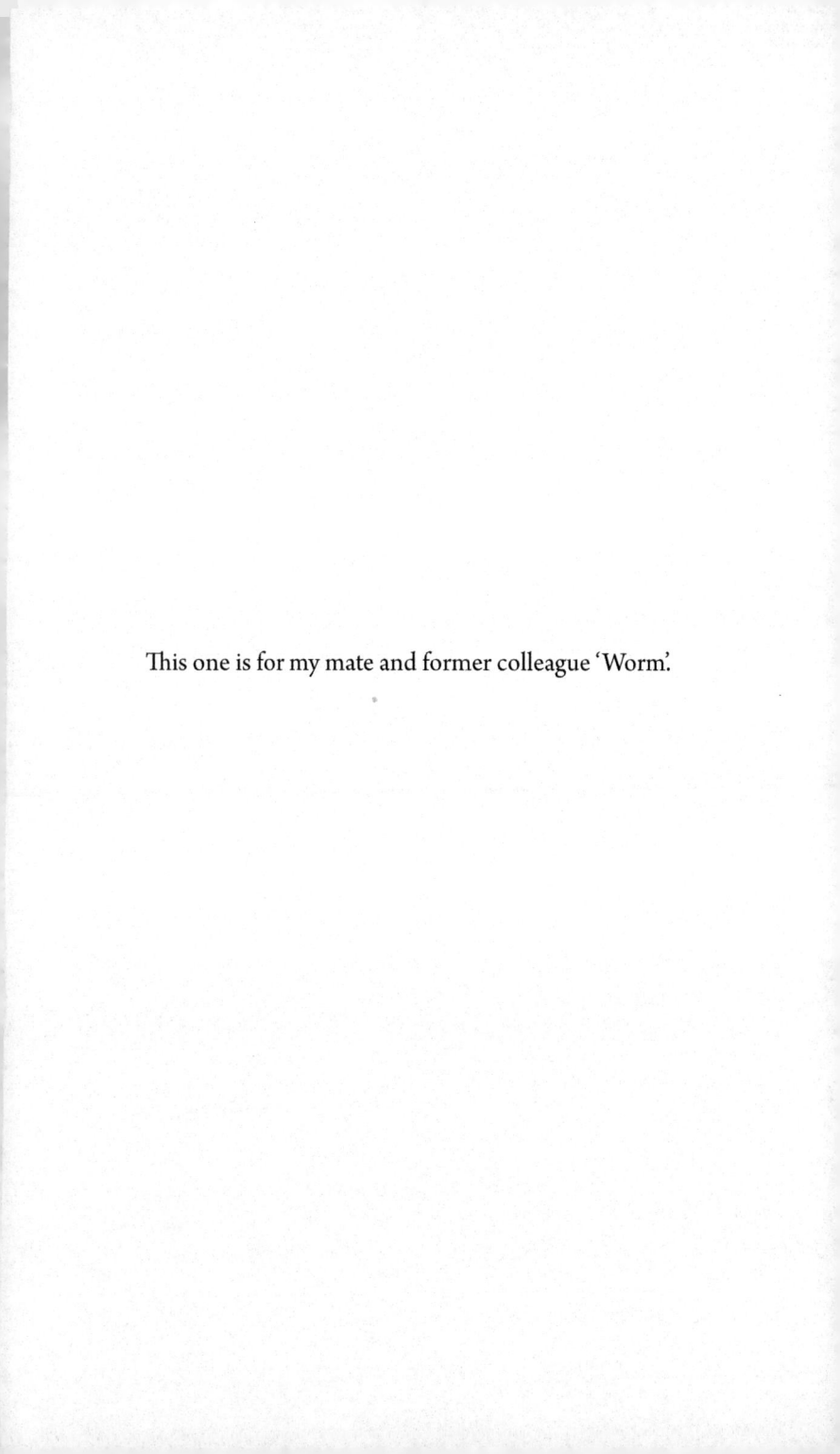

This one is for my mate and former colleague 'Worm'.

LITTLE DO YOU KNOW

PROLOGUE

The Present.

I COME HERE EVERY DAY.
I sit.
I watch.

For many people, they wouldn't do it. People are so busy with their lives. They don't take the time to sit and watch the world go by. Smell the fresh air on a windy day or embrace the cool change of the wind against their face.

I have important commitments. Just like everyone else. Yet I still find the time to open my camping chair and sit under the oak tree, in the middle of the botanical gardens. I just watch the world go by.

There are mothers with prams, or small children. On their way to the nearby museum or just using the park as a shortcut to head home. Joggers, runners, businesspeople, in their suits and ties. Families on holidays. Then there's the strange ones. The guy practising nun-chucks, or the woman trying to balance on her head. There's the homeless, carrying bags upon bags of belongings, or junk.

It's all walks of life. The park is a good place to sit and see a snapshot of what society has to offer. The normal. The weird. The desperate and the oblivious.

In summer, it's hot. The shade provides little protection from the heat and humidity. But I don't mind it. On the opposite end, winter is cold. It is typically my favourite season, because you can always wear some extra layers if need be. Protect yourself from the wind and an umbrella from the rain. Simple.

I've been coming here, on and off for eleven years. I started eleven years ago, then had a break for a long time. But now I've come back. The break that I had was out of my control. But that's okay. It's nice to be back. I can't dwell on the past.

I'm here now. That's all that matters.

It's important for me, to be here. For my own sanity.

Just to sit and watch the world go by.

It's also important because it's here where I'll find my next victim.

CHAPTER 1

The Past

Jock Dempsey looked down at his hands.

His black gloves were tight. He tried to make a clenched fist and felt the back of the material grabbing on his skin.

"You okay Mick?"

Jock glanced up, as he felt the pat on the back.

It was Benny.

Being embedded as an undercover operative in one of the most sinister drug syndicates in the history of Melbourne wasn't an easy feat. In fact, it was dark. Dark on the mind and dark on the soul. Yet some days, Benny made it easier. Who would have thought that a low-level, big-mouthed drug dealer would be a breath of fresh air in an otherwise mentally challenging environment?

Even though it had been three months, Jock still wasn't used to being called "Mick".

It still felt unnatural. Like everything else about this operation.

"Yeah fine," he responded, still clenching both fists in hope of stretching the gloves.

"You seem nervous?"

Jock glanced around. The small industrial shed was full of angry Serbians. Jock could count at least a dozen. He only knew about half of them. The other half were probably from out of town. Most were either getting changed into their war attire or picking and choosing their cache of weapons. It was like a scene from a bad Mexican drug cartel movie, without the Spanish.

"I always feel uneasy before a battle. You just never know if shit is gonna go wrong," Jock murmured. He didn't want to give off too much of the emotional unease that he was feeling.

Before Benny could speak again, a voice boomed from the entry.

"Listen up!"

Silence fell over the room. Everyone stopped what they were doing. All eyes were on the figure standing in shadow of the roller door. A big figure. Tall and stocky. He wore a black jumper and jeans. His ethnic appearance didn't match his name.

George.

He was the right-hand man to syndicate leader Nikola Petrovic.

George was an intimidating figure. Someone who rubbed Jock up the wrong way, and since their first encounter they had never gotten along. Jock tried many times, for the sake of the operation, but George had his wits about him and he smelt a rat. The trust was not mutual.

"Tonight, we're after Billy Jarman." George's voice boomed. "My people tell me he's staying the night at the Piranha's club house. There might be other people there, but we don't care. I want Jarman alive."

"Picking a fight with a motorcycle gang." Jock whispered. "Is this suicide?"

Benny sniggered. "They've obviously pissed off Nikola. He won't let this go."

George continued in his loud and authoritative voice. "Last week, Jarman thought it would be a good idea to kidnap and roll one of our boys. This doesn't go unpunished. We're leaving in ten minutes. Be ready."

Within a few minutes, Jock was whisked away into the backseat of a large SUV, sharing the seat with another hired goon. Not a word was spoken. His rear seat accomplice wasn't the 'chatty' type.

In the front, Benny sat in the passenger seat, the driver was George's close friend, Miroslav.

Jock had come to know Miroslav well. He was a long-time employee and loyal friend to Nikola. They attended school together back in Yugoslavia and eventually worked their way up to entrepreneurs. Businessmen. Except the wrong kind of business. Money laundering. Drug dealing. Sex trafficking. Anything that paid better than a traditional nine-to-five job.

Miroslav was well educated but didn't have the same charisma and leadership style that Nikola provided. Miroslav was the grunt. The engine room of the syndicate. He preferred to get his hands dirty, much like George. He'd rather let his physique do the talking.

"Where are the other cars going?" Benny quizzed.

Miroslav glanced across, glaring at him. "This your first rodeo Hill?"

Benny had a reputation of being the village idiot. So, the hierarchy nicknamed him "Hill" after the English comedian.

Jock sniggered.

"We always take separate routes. In case the pigs decide to stick their nose in. Then only one car gets picked off."

Benny nodded. Realising now how stupid his question was.

Jock glanced out of his window as their car slowly rolled up into a newly formed industrial estate in Port Melbourne. An area he should have been familiar with but had never seen before.

"Goran and I are going inside with George and his crew. Mick, you take the wheel. Benny, behave yourself and don't touch anything."

Jock nodded and glanced across at Benny, in time to catch the parting eye roll.

They approached a small industrial building. It had a traditional façade of a large roller door to one side and an office to the other. Floor to ceiling glass panels made up the office space with blinds drawn. It was well disguised to deter authorities from ever suspecting it as a front for a motorcycle gang.

Miroslav pointed across at a red utility parked on the street. "That's Jarman's car."

Before Jock could ask what their next move would be, two other vehicles pulled up alongside them. A passenger window lowered revealing George sitting in the passenger seat.

"Let's go," he barked.

Jock opened his door, racing around to the driver's seat in time to see Miroslav tear off to the front door with George and four other dark figures in tow. Within seconds, the door had been breached by a large ram and all the men disappeared inside. Guns drawn and ready for anything.

There was a short period of silence before the sound of men yelling; within moments two dark figures emerged dragging an unconscious male by the arms across to Jock's vehicle.

The rear door opened and the male was thrown into the backseat. Propped up alongside him were George and Miroslav.

"Drive," George said calmly, holding the male upright.

Jock threw the gear stick into reverse and drove out of the car park, before tearing back out the way they'd came in.

Jock peered into the rear-view mirror. Seated between George and Miroslav was a middle-aged man, bleeding from the nose and forehead. His face was unshaven, and he looked rough. Jock figured it must have been their target, given he was wearing his Piranha's motorcycle jacket.

"Head to the shipping yard," George instructed.

Jock nodded, swallowing hard. He could only imagine what was going to happen next.

Peering into his side mirrors, the two other vehicles were out of sight. They'd likely return to the office to pat each other on the back for a job well done.

As they neared the shipping yard, Jock pulled the car up to the boom gate. Glancing out of the window, he could see a security guard approaching with a clipboard.

"What now?" Jock asked, "what do you want me to do?"

"I don't want you to do anything," George barked, winding down his window.

The guard approached, and the expression on his face indicated to Jock that he'd been expecting them.

"Georgie!" the guard spoke jovially, "right on time."

"Thanks Andy," George responded, slipping something to the guard from the window.

"Keep the change," he added, throwing the guard a wink.

The guard smiled and nodded as Jock took that as his cue to continue driving into the shipping yard.

All around them stood shipping containers, some stacked

four or five high. The only light came from the full moon and the occasional spotlight overhead.

"Turn right when you pass that blue container, that'll do us," said George.

Jock peered across at Benny, noticing the beads of sweat on his forehead as he slowed the car down to a stop as instructed.

A dazed and confused Billy Jarman was thrown from the backseat by George. Hitting the ground with a thud, followed closely by a low groan.

"What now?" Jock asked.

"Stay in the car." George instructed angrily. Jock wasn't sure what to make of George's anger, whether it was the situation they found themselves in or Jock's persistent questions.

Jock wound his window up, just in time to shield out the noise of the flurry of punches and kicks that followed. Jarman was taking the brunt of George and Miroslav's size twelve boots.

Once they'd exhausted themselves, Jock watched on as George pulled a pair of garden shears from the back pocket of his jeans, wrapping the blades around Billy's index finger and without warning, pressed the handles together.

The sound of Billy's screams echoed throughout the container yard. Jock had seen his fair share of violence over the years, but this made his stomach churn. He looked over at Benny who was looking the other way, staring into the darkness.

"You know what we do to thieves?" George asked.

Billy rolled around on the concrete, clutching at his bloodied hand.

"Do you know who I am you fucking ignorant wogs?!" Billy squealed, "you're all fucked. I'm going to hunt you all down, one by one and kill all of you. Then send your severed heads to your families."

Jock shook his head. Billy was in no position to make threats and the men standing over him knew it too. George simply laughed, while Miroslav stood by, steely eyed. A look of resolve on his face.

George was the first to respond.

"It's going to be hard for you do that from a rubbish bag at the bottom of the bay now isn't it?"

Billy's breaths were shallow. He was trying to mask the pain, grimacing as he propped himself upright onto an elbow.

"So, what do you want from me?" he asked, in a calm voice. His spare hand gripping the stump that once was his index finger, trying to stop the bleeding.

"We don't like bikie's." George explained, twirling the garden shears around in his hand, "we certainly don't like the kind that forget their place."

"How do we fix this?" Billy murmured. He was pale. Sweating. Swaying. Looking as though he was about to vomit. It was evident he was doing a bad job of masking the shock that had set in.

Miroslav reached into his jacket pocket, retrieving a garbage bag. He tossed it about until it had filled with air and expanded.

"You can't fix this," George responded. "Where is our money?"

Billy shook his head. "Money's gone," he whispered.

"Wrong answer." George replied, turning his back.

As Billy followed George's movement's, he failed to see Miroslav approach from behind, slamming the bag over his head and pulling it tight.

Jock watched on as Billy struggled, attempting to fight for his life. His arms and legs thrashing about, gasping for air. A fight that Jock knew Billy would lose.

The Serbian's meant business. They weren't about to be intimidated by a local motorcycle gang.

Jock had come to understand quickly that the Melbourne underworld was like being in another country. Another planet even. It was a place where violence and intimidation ruled. Money meant everything. It was a place where only the strongest survived.

It was a bad horror show.

Jock had a front row seat.

CHAPTER 2

Jock glanced across at Benny. It was eerily quiet in Jock's car. Just the two of them. Reflecting on the events of the evening.

Although it was no longer evening but rather the early hours of the morning. Having returned to the garage and being debriefed by George, they didn't leave the shed until 2am.

Nikola's boys ensured that no one knew where Jarman's body would be dumped. It was better that way. The less people that knew, the less chance of anything coming back to the Serbians and more importantly, to Nikola.

"You haven't said much," Jock eventually spoke, slowing down for the red light.

Benny kept his eyes on the road. "They've never taken me along to anything like that before," he replied. "I've always just been Benny. The idiot that deals cocaine. I don't know why they asked me to come along."

Jock also had his reservations. Benny was good at his job, but that's where it ended. At only five foot five, and weighing no more than sixty kilograms, Benny looked like a junky and played the part well. He spent his spare time playing video games in his one-bedroom unit, that's when he wasn't peddling cocaine at nightclubs for Nikola.

That was Benny's 'thing' and had been for years. Never had George invited him along on to witness retribution. Perhaps it was a reminder of how powerful the Serbian family was. A reminder that everyone knew their place and what the consequences would be if they were double crossed.

"I wouldn't think too much about it," Jock replied. "They obviously have faith in you. They wouldn't ask you to do that shit if they didn't trust you to keep your mouth shut."

Benny's face dropped. "Or maybe they want me to blab. A reason to get rid of me."

Jock let out a snort. "If they wanted you gone, you'd be dead already."

Benny accepted Jock's logic with a smirk. But he still felt uneasy. He could feel it in the pit of his stomach.

"You keep looking in the rear vision mirror, everything okay?" Benny quizzed, glancing over his shoulder.

Jock slowed the car down, eventually turning right off the main road and into a side street. His eyes remaining on the mirror.

"What is it?"

Benny was getting nervous, bouncing his knees and constantly glancing over his shoulder.

"This car has been following us for the last fifteen minutes." Jock muttered, focusing on the road ahead.

Benny sat in silence. Uneasy. Jock didn't have to look across to read Benny's body language. He could see it from the corner of his eye.

"Relax. This is normal. Nikola has done this before."

"Why?" Benny asked.

"He keeps tabs on me. Don't worry, he would have done it to you too. You're just too stupid to notice."

Benny scoffed.

Jock made another right turn. Then another.

Without fail, the car continued to follow at a distance.

Jock drove the car back out onto the main road, eventually pulling into a 24-hour service station, parking alongside a bowser.

He glanced in the mirror, as the car in question followed, pulling up two bowsers over before coming to a stop.

"Watch this," Jock said, getting out of the car. Benny watched on as Jock wandered around to the opposite side of his car, removing the nozzle from the bowser.

They both watched on as a middle-aged man exited his vehicle, opting to do the same thing. Occasionally throwing Jock a sideways glance, attempting to not make it obvious.

Before Jock pressed down on the nozzle to release fuel, he returned it to the bowser, quickly making his way back into the driver's seat. His actions catching his would-be follower off guard.

Jock started the car and slammed down the accelerator, as the BMW screeched out of the service station and back out onto the main road.

Both men glanced in their mirrors, watching on as their stalker was left unprepared, nearly tripping over the petrol hose in his attempts to get back into his car. But it was clear from the view in the mirror, that they'd lost him.

"He didn't make it obvious did he?" Benny laughed, seemingly more relaxed.

Jock smiled. It was good to see Benny at ease again.

"This happens often?"

"At least once a week."

Benny shook his head. "Maybe I need to get out of this game. I'm paranoid as fuck. These guys are just messing with my head."

Jock glanced across and the worrying look had returned to Benny's face.

"Just do what your told. Don't go doing stupid shit and you'll be fine."

Jock pulled the car over outside Benny's unit. Leaving the car running in the street.

"Behave yourself. I'll see you later in the week," Jock instructed.

Benny nodded, closing his car door and pacing up the long drive, past the front units until he reached his own. Jock watched on, waiting until Benny was inside.

It was at that moment; his mobile phone rang.

Zoran's name lit up on the screen. He was Jock's undercover handler. Jock's only contact with the police force while the operation was running. His superior and more importantly his best friend.

"You've had an eventful evening," Zoran's voice was slightly distorted at the other end, "what did they do with Billy Jarman?"

"No idea," Jock replied, putting the car into gear and pulling away from the curb. "Shit just got real and the Inspector isn't going to like this. Doesn't pay to rip off the Serbs eh?"

"You know the Piranha's are going to retaliate. It's going to put you in the firing line now."

"They won't." Jock replied.

"How can you be sure?"

"They've cut the Piranha's off at the head. Jarman was

the Sergeant of Arms. I'm pretty certain that his finger is on its way to the rest of their crew with a note. They'd be stupid to fight back given they started this."

Jock could hear Zoran's sigh at the other end.

"For your sake, let's hope so."

CHAPTER 3

Present Day.

MELBOURNE'S INNER-CITY SUBURBS WERE DIAmonds in the rough.

Outside of the hustle and bustle of city life, Fitzroy proved to be a quiet refuge, just minutes from the city, where night-time revellers were staggering to find their way home on daybreak. Shift workers were commencing their early mornings on construction sites and eager white-collar workers were getting into town before the peak hour rush.

Jock's home was heritage listed and situated right in the centre of Fitzroy. Jasmine vines blanketed the façade, competing for sunlight with the red brick that lay beneath.

A home which he and his wife bought all those years ago, before the cost of buying a home now extended well beyond many peoples reach. Although now, all these years later, it was just Jock. With an occasional visitor.

An overnight visitor.

The beeping of the alarm on her iPhone was enough to startle Jade out of her deep sleep.

She rolled across and swiped up, hoping the noise hadn't woken Jock.

Peering across, his eyes remained closed and his breathing heavy. That was her cue. She slid back the doona and eased herself of his bed, trying not to make a sound.

Jade reached down and collected her pink shorts and white t-shirt from the floor. It was where they had ended up the previous night after a few glasses of red. The best merlot she'd had in a long time, and the headache she'd woken up with made sure she didn't forget.

"Where are you going?"

The murmur came from Jock's side of the bed and startled for the second time in as many minutes.

"Sorry, I didn't mean to wake you," she replied. Jade leaned back and glided her palm across his cheek.

"You don't have to go," Jock reminded her. "Lucy's not here till tonight."

"I know, but I have my first patient at quarter past nine, so I need to get ready and head into the office."

Being a psychologist had its perks. One, you could schedule patient appointments to suit your own calendar. Two, you could use perk one to get out of most uncomfortable situations. The patient appointment was straight from the textbook.

"I don't know how comfortable I would feel coming back here when your daughter is here," Jade added, "I haven't met her properly and I don't want her to think I'm just the booty call."

Jock let out a laugh, then propped himself up on his elbow. "Wasn't it you who said no strings attached?"

"I never said it was a bad thing," Jade smiled, "I just don't want to subject your children to our poor adult behaviour."

"She's hardly a child. The kid is 19. I'm sure she does the same thing."

Jade lifted herself up and out of the bed, sliding her t-shirt on.

"You often think of your daughter that way?" she said, smirking.

"What I'm trying to say is, she's not going to care," Jock responded. "Her mother probably does the same thing."

Jade's smile widened, "You said your ex was in a long-term relationship with another guy?"

"She is. But nothing to say she's not playing the field either."

"Like you do?"

"Steady on."

"I wasn't born yesterday. I know about the others."

"What others?"

"Last time I was here, I had to get my shoes from under your bed and found someone else's underwear."

Jock didn't embarrass easy, but he could feel his face turn a shade of pink.

"That was a long time ago," he replied, attempting to sweep her accusation away.

"That was two weeks ago John," Jade responded. She enjoyed making him squirm. "I don't care, I'm just saying. You're a horrible liar and you should start acting your age. Set an example for your daughter."

"You're one to talk," Jock scoffed.

Jade wandered around to his side of the bed and planted a kiss on his forehead. "You still okay for dinner on Sunday?" she asked.

"I'll have to check with the other women, but I think so."

Her kiss was closely followed by a jab to his arm. "Jerk."

Jock chuckled to himself as he watched Jade leave the

room, tilting his head to get a better view of her legs in those denim shorts.

He threw his head back onto the pillow and closed his eyes. Just five more minutes, then he'd consider heading into the office.

CHAPTER 4

The Present

That morning.

"THIS THIS IS YOUR DESK."

Blair couldn't help but stare inadvertently at his bosses belly. The buttons on his shirt were under immense pressure and looked as though they were going to burst at any moment. They would be a deadly weapon if they were to pop. A lethal projectile.

"Thanks Boss," he said, putting his backpack down on the empty desk.

"Please, call me Robbo. Everyone else does."

The Detective Senior Sergeant waddled away, puffing and heaving. His black curly hair bobbed up and down with each stride.

Blair looked around at his new surroundings. He had to pinch himself. The Homicide Squad had some prestige about it. It was the squad that most detectives aspired to work in and yet the selection system to get in came down to a lot of luck and who you knew. Being the son of a former Detective Senior Sergeant certainly helped Blair's cause. He'd only been in the force for six years and the last two years of that was doing temporary duties at the Melbourne Criminal Investigation Unit. Homicide would be his first official appointment. He knew it was rare, yet not impossible. The Chapman name was on his side.

He glanced around the room. What he expected to be an office full of activity, appeared to be dormant. The only people around were two analysts, tapping away on their keyboards. They were too engrossed in their work to look up from their screens.

Before Blair could open his bag, he heard a female voice approach.

"Detective Chapman? You must be Danny's kid?"

Blair turned in time to see a woman fast approaching, her hand outstretched as she prepared to greet him. She was dressed in a grey suit, wearing a pink shirt. Not a day over sixty, her face looked crisp, she'd obviously had some work done. She looked too sharp, neat and tidy to be part of the rank and file.

"Detective Inspector Pauline Evans," she added.

Blair shook her hand. He thought right. She wasn't rank and file. Her handshake had a firm grip.

"Yes, I am Danny's son," he muttered nervously.

"You look a lot like him. How is he these days? Enjoying retirement, no doubt?"

"He plays a lot of golf and babysits my niece and nephew. They keep him busy."

The Detective Inspector smiled. If anything, she was at least courteous and polite.

"Well, welcome to the team. It's great to have you on board. I believe you're in John's crew?"

"I think so," Blair replied, "I can only guess that's why I'm sitting over here."

"I believe they are out chasing up some loose ends, but they shouldn't be long. I have no doubt you've got your own work to get on with until they get back."

Blair simply nodded and returned the smile, going back to unpacking his bag. He watched on as Pauline disappeared back down the hall. She was much easier on the eye than he had remembered from watching her on television. Even for her age.

Just as Blair had pulled his seat back to sit down at his desk and admire his new surroundings, another figure emerged into the office. An older man, maybe mid-to-late fifties, he wore a blue suit and white shirt. His hair was dark, he was clean shaven, looking like the consummate professional.

No lanyard. No identification card.

Annoying, as this was the way you normally identified colleagues. Yellow card meant Detective. Green card meant someone of importance.

He had neither.

Blair watched on as the man fiddled with some papers on a desk, then rummaged through the drawer, then looked up, eventually making eye contact.

"You doing anything?" the man asked abruptly.

Blair shook his head.

"Good, come with me."

Blair got up, sliding his chair back under his desk. He grabbed his police diary and his pen, tucking it under his arm.

As he followed the figure down the hall, Blair decided to introduce himself.

"I'm Blair. Blair Chapman."

Blue suit continued walking, somewhat choosing to ignore Blair for a split second before he eventually responded.

"John Dempsey," came the reply. "My colleagues call me Jock. You can call me Detective Sergeant."

Blair nodded and smirked. Old school. He didn't mind the added attitude.

'This is why I'm here' he thought to himself, *'sit back and enjoy the ride'*.

CHAPTER 5

BLAIR LEANT FORWARD IN HIS CHAIR. THE INTERVIEW rooms at the Crime Department were nothing like the suburban stations. They were clean. Spotless in fact. The walls were free from carvings and graffiti. The tabletop glistened under the fluorescent lights above. Not a speck of dust or dirt. It probably had a lot to do with the fact they were barely used, Blair couldn't imagine people being interviewed for murder every day.

On the other side of the table sat a well-manicured male. He was dressed in a black polo and pale blue chinos, his hair slicked to one side. Not your traditional looking criminal.

They sat in silence. Blair didn't want to speak. He was only there to corroborate. He didn't want to get his new colleague off-side.

Within a few minutes, the door opened and Jock reappeared. This time without the suit jacket. His shirt sleeves were rolled up to his forearms, he carried a large binder, full of paperwork.

Jock quietly sat down and opened the binder. Inside it, Blair could see statement after statement, as he flipped through the paperwork. Then came the photos. Photos of a crime scene.

Images taken from camera footage. Photocopies of receipts. An entire investigation crammed into one binder.

Jock looked up and glared at Blair, before pointing to the digital recorder. It was a silent signal to restart the recording machine.

Blair nodded, pressing the button to recommence the interview.

Jock paused for a moment, before speaking. His voice monotone.

"Before we had a break earlier," Jock began, "you were telling me about how you and your daughter were sitting in the car having a snack of some description."

The man on the other side of the table felt obliged to answer. "Yes, that's right."

"You say this was a few hours after you and your wife had a disagreement and you walked out?"

"Yes."

Blair noticed the confident smirk on the man's face. He realised now that'd recognised him from the news. Arthur Herman. A local business owner whose wife had allegedly gone missing from their Hawthorn home after an argument. Blair recalled the story how she'd gone for a walk to get some space, then never came home.

He was suspected of having something to do with her disappearance. Since then, the story had gone cold. Blair now realising the Homicide Squad must have had at least some form of evidence, for him to be sitting in here, detained and answering questions.

"Would you say you have a good relationship with your kids Arthur?"

"Yes, that's right. The best. We are like best friends."

Jock pulled some paperwork from his binder, sliding it across the desk and laying it face up in front of him.

"Do best friends also deposit large sums of money into each other's accounts?"

Blair could make out the paper to be a bank statement.

Arthur appeared flushed, before recomposing himself to answer.

"The kids need cash from time to time. It's not like I don't have it to give them, so I help them out."

Jock nodded, sliding the paper back into the binder.

"Would you say this is a regular occurrence for your wife? To walk out after an argument?"

Arthur nodded, leaning forward in his chair, "she'd often leave, sometimes for hours at a time."

"So, you fought often then?"

Arthur's confident smirk returned. "You wanting to push me into a corner Detective? Yes, yes we did. But that doesn't mean I killed my wife."

Jock sat back in his chair, glaring at Arthur. The two of them staring at each other.

Jock eventually spoke. As he did so, he reached back into his binder to pull out yet another piece of paper.

"Arthur, you mentioned you were still at home after your wife left, is that right?"

Arthur nodded his head.

"And when did you say you left the house to pick up your eldest son?"

"Must have been around 8pm."

"Where did you collect him from?"

"Um, soccer training."

"Where was that?"

"Ah, let me think. Camberwell. The soccer grounds."

Jock slid the paper across the desk, placing it calmly in front of Arthur.

"Each telecommunications provider has mobile phone towers," Jock began. "These towers are spread out everywhere across the country. We find them in metro areas more commonly closer together. Whenever your phone sends or receives data, it finds the closest tower to your location. Not always, but most of the time. This piece of paper I've slid in front of you shows your phone history. It shows the data sent and received calls and text messages. On the day your wife left the family home."

Blair watched on as Arthur squirmed in his chair, scratching at his cheek.

"So, tell me Arthur, if you were in Camberwell at 8pm on the night your wife disappeared, why would your mobile phone be sending and receiving data from the mobile phone towers in Hurstbridge and Diamond Creek?"

Arthur was quick to respond, tapping his feet.

"Cause, um, phone transmissions aren't always accurate Detective. You just said it yourself. I'm not an idiot."

Jock picked up the piece of paper and slipped it back into the binder. He calmly sat back in his chair and crossed his legs.

"Arthur, you mentioned you were a smart guy. I don't doubt that for a second. You're very smart. I can see that. But let me fill you in a little bit about people who lie."

Arthur didn't respond. Instead, he sat back waiting for Jock's next move. The nervousness was written all over his face.

"What's not commonly known Arthur, is when the brain is under immense stress, the temperature rises and is exhibited by way of perspiration."

"Everyone sweats Detective. It's hot in here."

Jock's eyes narrowed.

"When you touch your face, it acts as a pacifier and has a calming effect to a brain that's under stress. Foot tapping is another sign of a brain under stress. These things happen when the brain must think on the spot, it works harder. You see Arthur, when I ask you a basic question, you can answer me with no hesitation. Yet when I ask you about a specific detail where I know you're lying, you move away from your baseline behaviour, and you stumble. You throw a few 'ah's' and 'um's' into your answers, you tap your feet. You rub your face. You purse your lips when I ask you a question where I know you're going to lie when you respond."

Having a friend with benefits who was also a psychologist was proving useful.

"Lying is far more mentally taxing then telling the truth Arthur. I can read you like a book. I've interviewed some of the most notorious murderers in this state in the last ten years, and you my friend are a rookie at this caper. I bet if I squeeze the kids, they'll at least be up front and honest with me do you think? Or will they sit there and squirm and hesitate and make up lies as they go along like you have been?"

Arthur's face flushed. He wanted to defend himself, yet he was speechless. He had nothing to say, and therefore felt it best to keep quiet. His facial expression was blank. He stopped squirming on Jock's observations. He was now very mindful of what he was doing.

Jock went on, "this morning, do you recall how we discussed the timeline of events? I asked you to run me through them."

Arthur looked down at the carpet before eventually replying, "no comment."

Jock leant across the desk and opened his diary to the last page of handwritten notes. Blair could see there was scribble written in blue pen, numbered from one onwards. It appeared as though it was a list. A list of Arthur's movements. A timeline.

Jock's eyes lit up and he turned his attention back to Arthur, the page of his diary still open. "Talk me through the timeline. Backwards."

Arthur's gazed remained on the floor. He began to twitch his fingers, rolling his thumbs around themselves.

There was a short moment of silence. Blair sat, eagerly waiting for Arthur to take the bait. To speak. To say something. Anything.

"Why do you want me to do that?" he eventually asked.

"Because if you're telling me the truth, you'll have no issues in reciting the timeline."

Arthur sat in silence again. Refusing to respond. He was now worried of incriminating himself further. Giving Jock further fuel.

"If you can't talk me through the timeline of your movements the day your wife disappeared, then how are you going to convince a jury?"

Silence.

Jock used this to his advantage. "So far Arthur, this recorded interview has shown the shifts in your body language and your inability to answer direct questions without stumbling. You're now refusing to take me through the timeline again. But this interview is just the beginning. Over the next few weeks, I'm going to find and download every piece of camera footage I can find between your house and your last known telephone ping. My team will download and analyse every form of electronic device you own, including those of your children. I'll apply for warrants to search your home and your business, collecting DNA from everything you own, everything your wife owned. My team and I won't stop until we have the truth seeing as we're not getting it from you."

Silence.

Jock continued, leaning forward on the desk again, his elbows firmly planted, "Or, you can tell me the truth right now."

Arthur shifted in his seat, using both his hands to prop himself upright. The perspiration still evident on his face.

"Okay," he replied eventually, an unusual croakiness to his voice. Tears began to well in his eyes, "it was an accident." He went on, lowering his head, "I got physical. I shouldn't have, but she pushed my buttons and I snapped."

Blair glanced across at Jock who had held his pose, still leaning forward on the desk.

Arthur's demeanour had changed. He had gone from arrogant and confident just moments ago; a man with a plan and a story to tell. Now, he was a shell of himself. He was sweating and nervous, in a state of emotional torment. It was as if a weight had been lifted from his shoulders as he now wept, rubbing away the tears from his face using the bottom of his shirt.

Jock sat back in his chair, relaxing his shoulders. "Tell me Arthur. Tell me everything that happened."

"That was really impressive," Blair eventually said, stirring the sugar into his mug, "It was so passive aggressive. Your technique. How do your interview methods normally go with the public prosecutor?"

Jock poured the hot water from the kettle into his mug.

"I don't interview crooks to appease the prosecution," Jock replied arrogantly, "I call it as I see it. He was nervous. He had something to hide, so I exposed it. It's up to the O.P.P now to make that work. My job is done."

He stirred his coffee, tapping the spoon against the mug and dropping it into the dishwasher.

Blair couldn't help but observe that Jock's interviewing technique and methods had completely gone against the grain of everything he had been taught, both in the academy and in detective training school. Yet it worked. Whether it worked well enough to beat a team of defence lawyers, time would tell.

As the two men wandered back into the muster room, a female voice called out from across the room.

"Dempsey," she called out over the partition, again. Glancing over at the two of them.

Tammy was short and stocky. Her thick black rimmed glasses suited her short blonde hair, as she leaned back in her chair, ushering for Jock to approach. She twirled in her pen in her hand with a confidence that suggested she had something useful to show him.

"What is it Tammy?" he mumbled, making his way over, trying hard not to spill his coffee.

Blair followed, curious to see what she had to show them.

"Did you know Silas Crowley got out of the bin a couple of weeks ago. I just went back over the prisoner releases and saw his name in the list."

"I did see that," Jock replied, letting out half a yawn. "Why do you mention it?"

Blair sensed a rudeness to his tone, yet Tammy smirked. Perhaps she was used to his odd behaviour. One thing was certain, they had some sort of strange bond. Maybe it came from working together for so long. Jock was dismissive of her and she was doing all she could to get him excited.

"I was looking through the active missing persons files

for the division and neighbouring divisions and just noticed a couple of interesting reports."

Tammy continued when Jock didn't respond.

"Two females, one aged 19, the other aged 21. Both reported missing in the last five days. Similar circumstances. Neither one returned home after a night out."

Jock peered over at her computer monitor, expecting to see the reports for himself.

"Tell me more."

"Sarah Stewart was the younger of the two. Narrative suggests she was out with friends at a Wine Bar in Prahran, left them around midnight. Lived locally and apparently walked home. Unsure if she got home, didn't turn up to work the next day. Reported missing by her boss. Local members attended her address and gained entry via the landlord. No sign of her and no sign of a struggle. Phone is switched off. Bank accounts not used. This was six days ago. Then yesterday, Kylie Ilevski, lives in Brunswick. Again, was out with friends. Her car is still where she parked it and boyfriend said she didn't come home. Friends said she left around 11.30pm. Last time they saw her. The catch is both girls were in the same areas at the same times."

Jock rubbed his chin, reading the narrative over Tammy's shoulder.

"What is Crowley's new address?" he asked.

"He's living in Carlton, renting an apartment. Seems too coincidental yeah?" Tammy asked, spinning her chair around to face him.

"Who's this Crowley guy?" Blair asked, leaning over the partition.

Tammy ignored his question, instead, waiting for Jock to respond.

"Can you set up a new investigation shell for those and

send me the details. I'll chase up the general duties members that took the reports."

"Will do," Tammy replied, swivelling back to face her computer.

"Oh, and Tammy? Good work." Jock muttered under his breath as he returned to his desk.

Tammy smiled and puffed out her chest.

"Grab your coat kid," Jock said to Blair, jotting down some quick notes in his diary. "We're going for a drive."

CHAPTER 6

"So, what's the deal with this info anyway?" Blair asked abruptly. He took hold of his seatbelt as Jock rounded the bend, the tyres struggling to keep their grip on the road.

Jock sat in silence for a moment as he navigated the busy afternoon rush of traffic along Alexandra Avenue. What was only an eight-kilometre trip was taking close to thirty minutes. Nothing unusual for peak traffic in Melbourne.

Eventually the reply came, after Jock mumbled something to himself about shit drivers.

"Silas Crowley," he began, before pausing again to run an amber light, "kidnapped four women around ten years ago."

"And you think it's him again?"

"It's no coincidence that this guy is released from prison and within a month we've had two reported missing women in as many days."

"What happened last time?" Blair asked.

"Aren't you a Detective?" Jock asked sarcastically. "You can figure it out."

Blair smirked and simply glared out his window. It took him a moment to swallow the sarcasm.

"You talk to all your colleagues like this?

Jock didn't flinch. Instead, keeping his eyes peeled to the road as they approached a red light.

"I don't talk to my colleagues. You being placed in my crew wasn't my decision kid."

"Yet, here we are," Blair replied, saluting him with two fingers.

Blair jerked back in his seat as Jock planted the accelerator as the lights changed.

Jock cleared his throat before continuing, opting to explain the story to shut his colleague up.

"In 2013, we had a series of missing persons files come through from general duties in the inner metro suburbs. At the time, I was transitioning from my role as an undercover operative back into the Crime Department. At that stage, we still had a Missing Persons Unit that was attached to the Homicide Squad. One of our tactical analysts whose job it was to check on the files on all new missing persons reports found the correlation. Young women, generally aged anywhere between 10 to 20 and generally after a night out with friends or relatives, wouldn't turn up to work or school the next day. Same M.O on each one. The women were never found. It was weird. Some of the victims were just kids which made us think it was potentially a kiddy-fiddling ring. But then a few were older teens. There was no logic to it."

"How did you work out it was Silas Crowley?"

"Someone called Crime Stoppers, anonymously. Had said Crowley would leave his house at around 10pm each night, particularly around the same days the girls went missing and wouldn't return home until early morning. That's how he came to be on our radar. We never knew who made the call, but it led us to him."

"What did he do for work?"

"He didn't work. Crowley was a loner. No family. No friends. He was on government benefits as he was classed as having a 'disability.' Autism of sorts. But he didn't fool anyone, he was a very intelligent man. He was methodical and had plenty of time to plan things out. He had every facet of what he was doing covered."

"So how did you work out it was him?"

"All circumstantial in the end," Jock replied. "We never found any direct evidence. Nothing ever linking him to the girls, except one girl. Dharma Curtis. 19-year-old from South Yarra. He was seen chatting her up outside a nightclub, only fifteen minutes before she was never seen again."

"You must have had more evidence than that?"

"We had some mobile phone data," Jock went on, "had pings of his phone within close proximity of each victim and around the same time the girls went missing. There wasn't much CCTV around back then. But then with Dharma's disappearance, a local convenience store had him following her down the street at one point. Not long before she was never seen again."

"You're shitting me?" Blair scoffed, "he was convicted by a jury on that?"

"Juries aren't always logical kid. They found him guilty on two of the four disappearances. He couldn't give us a conceivable reason why he was in those areas on those nights and he had no alibi. Like I said, circumstantial, but the prosecutors wanted to give it a go. It was made easier as there became a pattern to the disappearances, as soon as he was remanded in custody after his arrest, the disappearances stopped. The prosecution added that to their argument and must have convinced the jury."

"He went to jail?"

"He received a good sentence from the Judge. Ended up getting nine years, but only served seven and a half. By the time we got to trial, it was nearly eighteen months after the first girl went missing. He received a lengthy sentence because the girls were never seen or heard from again. Presumed dead. Bodies were never found and Crowley never gave up any information."

"Did he maintain he was innocent?"

"He never said a word. That was the weird thing."

"What do you think happened?" Blair asked.

Jock pulled up outside a wine bar on Williams Road, sliding into a no-standing zone and turning the engine off. The unmarked BMW's engine hummed to a complete silence.

He turned his body to face Blair.

"Honest opinion? No idea. But I did suspect he may have had help. There was never any evidence to suggest that, but it was just a gut feeling."

"You said he had no friends or relatives."

Jock stopped for a moment; hesitation written on his face.

"That's a story for another time. We need to get to work."

Blair nodded, unclipping his seatbelt.

They got out of the car and armed with their diaries and overcoats, they made their way to the last place Sarah Stewart was seen. 'Bruno's Wine & Pizza Bar.'

Jock bypassed the entry and wandered a couple of doors down. Glancing up at the overhanging ceilings of the nearby retailers. He glared up at the cameras of a nearby music store, as a homeless man wandered past them. The boombox in his shopping trolley pumping with 80's tunes as he mumbled to himself. Across the road, prams were being pushed by mothers, with small toddlers in toe. It was the usual Tuesday afternoon.

The traffic around them was chaotic, as it was nearing peak hour.

"Can I help you boys?" a voice muttered behind them.

Out of one of the shop fronts, an older Italian man appeared standing in the doorway of Bruno's. His balding head was overshadowed by the creases on his face.

"You own this place?" Blair quizzed.

Before the man could respond, Jock stepped forward and with his arms open wide, embracing the old Italian man with a hug.

"How have you been you old bastard?" Jock asked smiling.

"Haven't seen you for a long time Johnny," Bruno replied with a raging grin, from ear to ear. "You no come here no more."

"Yes, it's been a while my old friend," Jock replied, "and while we come to reminisce, I'm going to need to see your camera footage from the weekend."

Blair paced up and down the restaurant. His hands intertwined behind his back, glancing down at the lino floors. He'd been locked out of the discussions between Jock and his old acquaintance. That came as no surprise.

Peering down at his watch, it was well past the time he'd normally be heading home. He knew homicide life would be long days, but he didn't realise it would be every day. His partner certainly didn't seem fazed by it.

Blair turned on his heels to hear laughter as the two men emerged from Bruno's small office. Jock with his hand on Bruno's shoulder.

"How is your son going?"

Bruno's expression changed from jovial to sadness almost within an instant. "He's not doing well Johnny," he responded, "I don't know how much longer we'll have."

Jock stopped, taking a quick sideways glance over at Blair, he spoke again, his voice lowered so Blair couldn't hear him.

"I'll get some money together for you," Jock muttered, "give me a few days okay? He needs that treatment, and you make sure he gets it."

Blair turned to peer out of the windows, attempting to be discreet and give the two men some privacy. As he glanced down to check the time again, he heard the door open and watched on as a large solid man appeared in the doorway. He was unsteady on his feet and the stench of alcohol was rampant.

His black trackpants were well worn and his hooded top was covered in stains. For a short moment, Blair thought perhaps he knew Bruno and that's why he'd entered.

"You open? I want a pizza." The man blurted out abruptly. He glanced over at Blair, sizing him up and taking in the corporate attire and equipment belt before eventually smirking.

"We don't open on Monday's," Bruno replied, "Sorry. Maybe come back tomorrow."

The man took another look at Blair, before peering over at Jock. Still swaying and unsteady on his feet.

"So, I guess the pigs just get special service then?"

Jock took a step forward. "What did you say hero?"

The uninvited guest didn't move, holding his ground.

He stood further upright. He attempted to suck in his stomach and puff out his chest, lifting him another inch off the ground.

"You heard me pig. What gives you the right? You think you're better than the rest of us. You can just help yourself eh?"

Before Blair could even formulate a plan on how to handle the uninvited guest, Jock had already launched, delivering a flat palm to the man's sternum before pouncing and catching him off guard. He had him in a headlock, squeezing his forearm against the man's neck.

"That was very rude of you," Jock muttered into the man's ear. "You apologise to Bruno. It's not his fault you're an ignorant piece of shit."

Blair watched on as the man's face began turning purple, he was flopping his arms about helplessly.

"Sorry," he whispered through his pursed lips, regaining some color in his face as Jock loosened his grip.

"Call the local boys," Jock barked at his partner. "They can come and get this idiot and he can spend some time in the cells."

Blair unclipped his radio from his belt. He called for the local members to assist and watched on, as Jock dragged his compliant offender from the restaurant foyer out onto the footpath. The man's feet dragging along the ground behind his body, still entangled in Jock's grip.

Jock lent in again, whispering into the man's ear, "don't you ever speak to me like that again."

"How do you know Bruno?" Blair asked, clipping his seat

belt into place. With Jock's driving, there was no hesitation. He was still amused by Jock's reaction to the abusive customer that had wandered into Bruno's shop.

Jock glanced into his blind spot, before pulling the BMW out of the parking bay and back into peak hour traffic.

"I've helped him out a few times over the years," Jock replied. "He's a nice guy, just trying to make an honest buck."

Blair accepted his reply. As Jock accelerated away from the traffic lights, his phone hummed away in his pocket, eventually emitting a loud dial tone through the car speakers.

Jock blushed, almost embarrassed at the commotion his phone had caused. He pressed the pick-up button on the steering wheel.

"John Dempsey," he answered.

A female voice spoke nervously at the other end.

"Jock. It's Penny."

Blair glanced across at his counterpart, who's face had now gone from pink to red.

A female caller. Blair sensed the call had caught his partner off guard.

"Now's not a good time," Jock replied. "I've got someone else in the car with me and I'm on my way to a job."

"That's what I was calling about," she quickly responded, "I wanted to talk to you about Silas Crowley getting out. Maybe do a follow up piece."

Blair shook his head. Penny wreaked of being a journalist.

"I don't think it's worthwhile Penny," Jock replied casually, "time to move on from Silas. I think there's bigger stories out there right now."

"Anything you're working on at the moment that I could maybe use?"

Jock shook his head. He looked across at Blair who was smirking.

"Can I call you later?" Jock asked.

"Sure. But if you have something for me, remember I have a deadline."

"Give me an hour."

Jock pressed the button on the steering wheel to end the call. There was a moment of silence before Blair opted to interrogate his partner.

"Is that Penelope Acres? From the Melbourne Herald?"

"Ten points for you," Jock replied sarcastically. "She's a good friend. That's it."

As Blair peered out of his window as Jock's phone rang again. The Inspector's name flashed up on the dashboard.

"Fuck," Jock muttered, answering the phone again. The Inspectors voice beaming through the car speakers.

"John, where are you?"

"Driving around Melbourne," he replied, continuing his run of sarcasm with a new audience. "What can I do for you boss?"

"I just had a call from a Sergeant at Prahan," she began. "Did you give them a drunk to lodge?"

"Red hot," Jock mumbled, looking across at Blair, "Yes boss. He abused us while we were getting some footage. And he was pissed," Jock explained.

"He has some bruising on his neck. The Sergeant wants you to give her a call." The Inspector explained. "Make this go away John. I don't need a Detective Sergeant in my crew with a silly little complaint hanging over his head."

Jock pressed the hang up button on the steering wheel.

"For fuck's sake," he muttered to himself, glancing over

at Blair. "That took less than half an hour. I bet she's a new Sergeant too. Needs a scalp to add to her resume."

Blair laughed, before Jock continued. "I'll call her when we get back to the office, but if she asks, he put up a fight."

Blair glanced back at him, "Sure thing," he replied. He wasn't going to argue with his new Sergeant. Not if he wanted to keep his spot in the team.

"What's the plan of attack from here?" he asked, changing the subject.

Jock took a moment to reply, as he turned off the main road and into a side street.

"We're going to pay Silas Crowley a visit."

CHAPTER 7

The Past

THE MUSIC IN THE NIGHTCLUB WAS PUMPING LOUDER than usual. New DJ or perhaps a new speaker system. Jock couldn't work it out. He glanced sideways at Benny. The perspiration on his face was clear that he was always nervous in the boss' presence.

"Where's Nikola?" Jock yelled, over the top of the music.

Benny glanced across. "He said he'd meet us here."

Jock peered around the room, taking in his surroundings. He'd be at least twenty years older than most of the patrons in there. The ground floor was for the kids peddling fake ID's and short skirts. Jock knew the mezzanine floor was for Nikola's 'special' guests. Generally reserved for guests on his payroll or high rollers that would be happy paying for top shelf whiskey and somewhere they could bring their girlfriends while their wives slept at home.

Carly Rae Jepson had just finished on the speaker system as the DJ transitioned his beats into a remixed version of Diamonds by Rihanna.

Within a few moments, a figure emerged in an expensive suit. Slicked black hair, short facial stubble, neatly groomed. He wore a white shirt with cuff links protruding from the sleeves. He was closely followed by an entourage, in which Jock instantly recognised as George and Miroslav. Jock had to swallow his smirk as he watched them walk in; it was as if they were carrying watermelons under each arm.

"Gentlemen," Nikola greeted them, shaking both their hands, "come along, follow me upstairs."

Jock and Benny followed the others as they made their way through the dance floor to a flight of stairs, which took them one flight up to the mezzanine. Jock had heard a lot about this club from friends, but he was yet to visit. It was invitation only, even for staff of the Serbian underworld.

From the mezzanine, George led them through an internal door and into what looked like a private room. It was filled with cigar smoke, whiskey glasses and men dressed in suits. They were surrounded by topless female bartenders and large Maori security staff.

Jock felt as though the nightclub had suddenly transformed into a men's gallery. Or a meat market. It was difficult to distinguish the difference.

"What do you think gentlemen?" Nikola asked, a grin from ear to ear, "fancy a drink?"

George ushered to one of the female bartenders, who acknowledged his motions with a nod, before pouring out three glasses of a top shelf scotch.

Jock kept his eyes on Nikola, watching as he scanned the room, the smile still evident on his face. He was proud of his new club and even more impressed that the private room was filled with guests with relatively large wallets.

"Come," Nikola continued, waving his hand at them, "there is someone you need to meet."

Jock and Benny followed Nikola and his sidekicks, filing

through the crowd, before they reached the corner of the room. That was when Jock realised who Nikola had bought them over to see.

Two men sat on a three-seater couch, separated by a semi-naked woman in-between. Both men were trying their hardest to keep their drinks upright, while keeping a grip on the women sitting on their laps.

Jock recognised the man seated on the right. Owen Hansen. The Minister for Police.

The other appeared to be another politician, Brad Bridges. It was lost on Jock who he was, but he knew he had a portfolio of some description under the current serving government.

Both men would be on Nikola's payroll. There was no doubt in Jock's mind. Their eyes like dinner plates and glancing down at the glass coffee table at his feet, Jock couldn't mistake the white powder and rolled up fifty dollar notes for anything other than a good time.

"Minister's," Jock said, nodding his head in greeting. It was the only way he could pass on what he was looking at to Zoran who was on the other end of Jock's communications, listening in to the events unfolding as he always did as Jocks' handler. Ready to step in if things went south.

Neither man flinched. They were both high and oblivious to the small crowd gathered around them. Benny meanwhile was perspiring harder than usual. The sweat dripping off the edge of his nose.

"What the hell is wrong with you?" Jock muttered at Benny, behind gritted teeth.

Benny shook it off. Now wasn't the time.

"They are obviously busy men," Nikola laughed, dismissing the two politicians, "yet they both helped make this possible. It is because of them we were able to get this club open."

George passed the freshly poured drinks around and Nikola raised his glass. "To opening night, and many more like it."

Jock and Benny acknowledged Nikola's toast and they all downed their double shots.

The drink didn't appear to relax Benny's nerves. He squeezed his eyes shut. Nikola laughing at him, thinking it was just Benny unable to hold his liquor.

Jock swallowed hard. Benny's behaviour was a shadow of something he couldn't quite read. There appeared to be a flicker of guilt on his face, which would explain the excessive perspiration. But Jock had no idea what it was.

"Now," Nikola continued, "let's head outside, we have other matters to discuss."

They all followed George and the entourage out through a doorway and down a flight of stairs, which opened up into the laneway behind the club. A cobblestone dead end road with parked cars and a dumpster.

As the door opened, the sound of the music began to fade, and Jock felt his ear drums once again relax. A light drizzle had begun to set in as they stepped out onto the road, directly into a black Hummer parked outside.

Nikola, being the last one outside, closed the door behind him. He brushed past Jock and made his approach toward Benny.

"Benny," he began, "what's this about you sniffing around asking questions about matters that don't concern you?"

Jock looked across in dismay. There was no warning for the anticipated confrontation and suddenly Benny's heightened nerves began to make sense to him. There was a tone of frustration in Nikola's voice.

"Nothing Boss," Benny stuttered, "I was just asking for a friend."

"What friend?"

Nikola stood still, arms by his sides. Chest puffed out. They weren't moving past this topic, not without answers.

"It's nothing Boss," Benny repeated, "honest mistake. I didn't mean to pry. I just sell drugs and my business has nothing to do with these women."

Nikola rolled his head around his shoulders.

"Now, Benny. You know that everyone has a job to do and no one deviates from those jobs. It's why everyone gets paid good money. Like George and Mick here."

"Yes yes," Benny replied frantically, "I know. I know. As I said, I didn't mean to stick my nose in. I'm sorry."

Jock knew from the time he'd spent working within the syndicate that Nikola was very private about his business. Everyone had a task and a network, and this process doesn't change. Although it was the first time he'd heard Benny sniffing around the group, asking questions about some women? Was it a trafficking ring? It was the first Jock had heard of this.

"What I do with the rest of my business, has nothing to do with you," Nikola said, raising his voice. It was short and sharp. Direct. George stood close by his side, cracking his knuckles.

Jock could sense the heightened hostility. He wanted to intervene, but he knew he'd be risking his own life. He had to shake it off, realise this was reality and Benny wasn't worth it.. He was a crook after all, a drug dealer. What Benny got himself into was Benny's responsibility. Not Jock's. He lowered his head, glaring at the ground. He knew what was coming for Benny. It was inevitable. Everyone in this group was indispensable. Everyone could be replaced.

Nikola stopped for a moment and glanced around the

street, before eventually ushering Jock toward the car. "Mick, after you."

Jock looked at Benny. The terror was evident on his face. If Benny could speak right now, he'd be begging for Jock not to get in that car. Not to leave him there. Alone with Nikola's men.

"Let's go," Nikola repeated, raising his voice and ushering his palm onto Jock's back.

Jock took one last look at Benny and climbed into the back seat of the car, moving across to the opposite side. Nikola climbed in after him and within a few moments, the door had been closed and the car was on the move. Jock peered out of the tinted windows. City lights surrounded them as they pulled out onto Flinders Street.

He glanced out of the back window, in time to see George approach Benny, and within a few seconds, the light drizzle of rain had turned into a heavy downpour.

The sound of the rain would not be enough to drown out the sound of what followed.

The sound of the single gun shot.

Jock sat in silence. Neither he, nor Nikola spoke a word. That was until the car pulled up outside the Crown Towers Hotel. No surprise to Jock; it was likely that this was Nikola's temporary home. Jock knew that Nikola had a house in Toorak. He'd driven past it from time to time, dropping off parcels.

The back door opened and a man in black pants and a maroon vest ushered them out.

"Do you have any bags Sir?" the man asked.

"Not today." Nikola responded. "My driver will park it in the usual spot."

The man acknowledged Nikola with a nod and walked away, ready for the next guest.

"Upstairs," Nikola said, pointing his index finger and ushering Jock into the building and into the lift, where he pushed the button for the 37th floor. The penthouse suite. Once again, no surprise.

They didn't speak another word as the lift jolted into motion, delivering them to the top floor within a matter of moments, not stopping for any other hotel patrons.

Jock still trying to process what had just unfolded. He didn't want to say anything to alert Nikola to the open phone line connecting him with Zoran. Everything would eventually play out in due course and Jock knew he'd have a chance soon enough. This was all part of the job. There were always risks.

The lift let out it's pleasant arrival tone as it came to a halt and the doors opened. Jock following Nikola down the hallway to a set of double doors. In the ten months Jock had 'worked' for the Serbian's, he'd never been invited, nor stepped foot, into any of Nikola's private dwellings.

As Nikola unlocked the doors, they opened out into a large suite, filled with expensive furniture, thick drapes and a view to die for. The city lights lit up the room before Nikola hit the switch for the pendant lights that illuminated the bar.

"Can I get you another drink?" he asked politely.

Jock shook his head.

"Suit yourself," Nikola continued, popping the lid from a crystal bottle and pouring its amber contents into a matching glass.

"Take a seat."

Jock was amazed by the surroundings. Floor to ceiling mirrors captured most of the city surrounds and a near one-hundred-and-eighty-degree panoramic shot. The only thing blocking out the skyline were the white sheers which draped from the ceiling. Expensive views. All paid for by drug money.

Jock sat himself down on the couch, choosing the end. He was nervous, unsure of what the next phase of the conversation would bring. The fact Nikola had no entourage with him kept his mind at ease. Nikola rarely did his own dirty work, so the possibility of being shot was the last thing on his mind.

"What did Benny tell you?"

Nikola was getting straight to the point.

"Honestly?" Jock asked. "Nothing at all. It's the first I've heard of it."

Jock's answer seemed to appease Nikola. He nodded and took a sip of his drink. Running his index finger around the rim as he lowered it back down into his lap, keeping his eyes on Jock.

"You see," he began, "I never liked Benny. He was a noisy little shit. Prying his nose into things that didn't concern him. And I had my suspicions that he was stealing from me."

"He had it coming then huh?" Jock tried his hand at humour, but it came across seemingly awkward. Nikola didn't respond. His facial expression remained cold.

"Tell me again where you grew up?" Nikola asked.

Jock shifted in his seat awkwardly.

"Sydney." Jock replied. "Manly to be exact."

"Who were your parents?"

"Beth and John. Mum was a pharmacy assistant. Dad worked driving the sea ferries."

Nikola nodded, taking another sip of his drink.

"How did you come into money again?"

"A good friend of mine growing up, he grew a crop out in the western suburbs, in a few different houses. I was selling for him. Eventually I went out on my own."

"What was your friends name?"

"Eric."

"Tell me more about this business?"

"I made some connections. Began moving heroin. Then got raided by the cops. I did two years in prison before I got out and that's when I moved to Melbourne. To start again."

Nikola nodded approvingly.

"Show me your driver's licence."

Jock reached into his back pocket, pulling out his wallet. He slid out his licence. A fake, in the name of Michael Murphy. He passed it over to Nikola.

"Bank card?"

Jock opened his wallet again. Another card in the name of Michael Murphy. Thankfully he was prepared. That was one thing the police force did right. The identity and the cover stories were generally very well thought out and executed. They had to be. There would be too great a risk if they weren't done properly. In the modern age of technology, everything could be found digitally quite quickly.

He passed it across, then watched on as Nikola took out his mobile phone and took a photo of both cards, before tapping away at his screen and eventually handing them back to Jock.

Nikola continued on his phone as Jock slipped his wallet back into his pants. He sat in silence for a moment, now understanding what it was like being on the other end of an interrogation.

Except this one could cost him his life if his cover was blown. He was trying not to squirm in his seat.

"Won't be long," Nikola reassured him. Still glaring at his phone.

Jock sat, wondering who the photo had been sent to.

As they continued in their moment of silence, Jock

couldn't help but glance outside. The balcony looked just as impressive as the rest of the penthouse. It stretched the entire length of the building. Nikola kept his gaze, twirling the amber liquid in his crystal glass. Jock felt uneasy but couldn't show it. Any hint of nervousness would likely destroy the relationship that he'd taken nearly two years to build with Nikola and exploit him as being a fake.

Within a few minutes, Nikola's phone beeped and both men were alerted to the notification.

"Okay." Nikola eventually said, after what felt like an eternity of them sitting in silence. He had slipped his phone down onto the coffee table after studying the screen for a short moment.

It appeared to be the news he was looking for and now he seemed more relaxed. Jock could feel his racing heart ease. Thankfully his back story had worked.

"You've been working for us for a while now," Nikola began, "and now I'm a man down, so I'll need you to step up. Good help is hard to find unfortunately."

Jock nodded, "I agree."

"As I said," Nikola continued, "I never liked Benny. His profits were always coming back short. Then he started snooping around in business that didn't concern him. He was, however, keeping my high rolling clients happy."

Nikola took another sip of his drink, rubbing his hand down his thigh, "Politicians. Celebrities. People in places of power. People that I need. This will now be your role."

"Who are we talking?"

"You'll see in due course," Nikola answered. "My team will provide my clients with your details. They will make contact with you when they need something. You will cater for their needs. I don't like unhappy customers. It's bad for business.

Unhappy customers can mean problems for me, which then means problems for you."

Jock nodded.

"You do this for me, you'll be rewarded accordingly."

Before Nikola spoke again, George entered the room, clutching at a hand towel, drying his hands. Jock was wondering how long George had been there. Obviously long enough to come in quietly and clean himself up.

"We're done here," Nikola exclaimed, getting up off the couch. "Your timing is perfect George, can you please show Mick out?"

Jock stood up and made his way to the door, refusing to look back. He stood by the handle, waiting until George approached from behind.

Without warning, Jock felt a blow to the back of his legs, sending him to his knees. The force of the blow buckling his legs.

He felt an enormous hand grab the back of his collar, lifting him back to his feet.

"Don't fuck this up!" George whispered, breathing into Jock's ear, "or you'll end up with Benny."

CHAPTER 8

The Present

A S THEY STOOD OUTSIDE THE HOME OF SILOS Crowley, Blair took in his surroundings.

It appeared a relatively normal neighbourhood. Quiet.

Nothing to suggest a convicted criminal was living in the street.

The house was relatively modern, built mainly of dark blue bricks and black window trimmings. The garden was well kept and manicured. Almost as if an old lady had lived there.

Blair immediately noticed there were no cars at the property.

As the two of them approached the front door, Jock grabbed his partner by the jacket, pulling him in close. Blair could feel Jock's breath on his cheek. The mixed smell of residual coffee and chewing gum.

"Don't say a word to this bloke," Jock muttered. "Let me do the talking. Don't say anything and don't DO anything. I don't want you to fuck this up. This guy is a lunatic. He'll push your buttons and I don't want you to take the bait."

Blair nodded. He hadn't seen Jock this serious and

he certainly had an element of intimidation to his tone. "Understood." Blair replied.

Jock let go and climbed the single step up to the open front door. Silas Crowley was already there, waiting for them.

Blair could make out his shadow in the doorway. He had long black hair, nearly shoulder length. It appeared wet and shiny. It complimented the facial stubble and weathered face.

"Mister Dempsey," Silas greeted him, a croakiness to his voice. He spoke with a cool and crisp monotone. He looked everything like the creep that Jock had described and he sounded like one too.

"Silas," Jock replied, "I heard you were out."

"It didn't take you long to find me detective," Silas added. "To what do I owe this pleasure?"

"How did you enjoy your time in prison?" Jock asked, smirking.

"If you came here to antagonise me detective, you've wasted the trip. If you must know, I spent most of my time reading, studying law and psychology so it wasn't all bad. I should thank you actually for putting me there. It was the time away I needed. To rest and reset."

"I'm glad to hear you enjoyed it then," Jock added. "Was all that reading to help you study preventions on being caught next time?"

"There won't be a next time detective. I'm a changed man. I've turned to God. Jesus. Our lord and saviour."

Silas grin widened, exposing a row of decayed teeth. Jock could sense Silas' sarcasm.

"Don't be angry detective. It's okay that you never found all those women. They'll turn up in due course. Patience is the key."

Jock gritted his teeth. Rubbing his jaw from side to side.

"You back to old tricks again Crowley?" He asked, composing himself.

"Whatever do you mean detective?"

"Sarah Stewart. She went missing two nights ago. Has your calling card all over it."

"I don't know what you mean Mister Dempsey. But I hope she turns up. For your sake." Silas teased.

Jock turned to Blair. "Can you give us a moment?"

Blair, squinting to keep the sun from his eyes nodded and wandered back to the police car.

"Your partner is very handsome Detective. I thought you worked alone. Or has something changed in the last ten years that I've been away?"

Jock took a step in toward Silas. He was close enough to see the loose brows of hair embedded within his eyebrows, growing in different directions. Jock kept his voice low. "You'd better start sleeping with one eye open Crowley," he began, "because I'm going to kill you. I'll be here one day when you least expect it and I'll finish you, like I should have done a decade ago. You're a cockroach and an oxygen thief and I'm going to make sure you don't hurt another person."

Silas took a step back, his grin widened. It was as if he was enjoying the threat.

"Now now Detective. That's no way to treat a man who's done his time. But I sure hope you pop by again soon, because nothing thrills me more than to see you. It brings joy to my day."

Silas pouted his lips and blew Jock a kiss before retreating into his home, closing the door.

Jock glanced at the front door for a short moment, before wandering back to the car, peering up and down the street.

"Cameras across the road too," Blair added, seemingly knowing what Jock was looking for.

The two men opened their doors.

"What are you thinking?" Blair asked.

"I'm thinking he's picked up where he left off," Jock replied, "and I'm going to do everything I can to prove it."

The drive back to the office was a long one. Peak hour combined with a multi-car pileup ensured Jock and Blair would be spending more quality time together. More than they had anticipated.

"What did you say to him?" Blair asked, glaring out his window.

"I told him I was watching him," Jock lied. "That I'd know what he was up to."

"Do you really think he's responsible? Would he be that stupid to do it all again?"

Jock scoffed and Blair caught the tail end of his eye roll. "I didn't come down in the last shower," Jock responded. "If it walks like a duck and quacks like a duck, chances are it's a duck."

"What happened to all those victims last time?" Blair quizzed.

"We don't know."

Blair squirmed in his seat. "Do you think it was bigger than just Crowley? You know how you hear about those pedo rings, how they move kids around-"

Jock took a moment to glance across at his colleague. "You've been talking to your old man haven't you?"

Blair could feel his face flushing red. He didn't want to appear as though he was going behind Jock's back.

"He may have brought it up, a long time ago, that's all. I remember him talking about Silas Crowley. The Serbs too."

Jock wriggled in his seat. It had been a while since anyone had bought up his history. Particularly someone he barely knew.

The connection between his past and his present seemed as evident now as ever before.

"Your old man was a good cop," Jock replied. "He came in and mopped up what we weren't allowed to finish. But whatever he's told you, it's only half the story. With all respect to your dad, he didn't get involved until the end."

"Why don't you enlighten me with the rest of the story? Your version." Blair asked genuinely.

Jock simply gave him a sideways glance. "Maybe another day."

Blair logged off his PC, picking up the last of his uneaten lunch and slipping it back into his backpack.

The office was buzzing with detectives. It was close to 6pm, and most who were on day shift were ready to pack up and head home for the day. Some opted to stay, with work still to be done.

A female colleague glanced across at Blair, forcing eye contact, before making her way over, manoeuvring her way between the desks.

"Hi, I'm Katrina," she eventually said, slipping Blair an outstretched hand. "You the new guy?"

Blair shook her hand. For a small petite woman, she had an awfully strong grip.

"Blair. Blair Chapman," he replied. "Yeah sort of new. Just here on temporary duties. Hoping to maybe get a spot at some stage."

Katrina screwed up her face. A puzzled look, before her shoulders eventually lifted, "Oh, you're Dan's son? I've heard a lot about you."

"Only good things I hope?"

"Your dad was a great boss," she continued, "pity he retired when he did. Replaced by the new generation of 'squeezers.' Your dad was old school. We all enjoyed working with him."

Blair nodded, slipping his backpack over his shoulders and zipping up his jacket.

"Hey listen-"Katrina continued, "a few of us are just popping out for a quick beer. If you're not doing anything, you're welcome to join us?"

Before Blair could respond, another male approached, propping himself up on the desk beside Katrina. He was tall with an olive complexion. He looked sharp in his suit, but more like a body builder than a detective. He was big and burley and he passed his hand through his wavy brown hair, seemingly trying to emulate a shampoo commercial.

"You must be Junior," he said with a deep voice, outstretching his hand but opting for a fist pump instead. "I'm Marcus, just a senior demon like the rest of the peasants on this floor."

Despite Blair only being a Detective for a short time, he knew the term 'Senior Demon' referred to detective senior constable. A term rarely used by the next generation of police. It proved that Marcus was not new. He'd been around, despite looking relatively young.

"That's me," Blair eventually replied, "Blair Chapman. Nice to meet you."

"How is it working with the nut case?" Marcus quizzed. He nodded in the direction of Jock who was standing by the printer, pressing an array of buttons and cursing under his breath.

"Dempsey? He's okay. Set in his way a bit." Blair responded diplomatically.

"We're meant to be part of his crew," Marcus added. "He's our detective sergeant, although you wouldn't know it. He doesn't normally give a shit what we do. You're going to love this crew if you end up on it, but you need to keep away from Dempsey. He's bad news."

"Thanks," Blair responded, "I'll keep that in mind."

"You coming for a beer?"

Blair glanced across at Jock, who was still hypnotised by his printing saga.

"You know what? I might just take you up on that offer."

As Blair lowered his backpack against the edge of the bar, he took a glance around the room. He expected it to be busier for a Friday night. Perhaps the presence of a few off-duty detectives hunting in packs within the pub helped clear out the unwanted patrons.

Before Blair could sit down, he heard a familiar female voice behind him.

"What will you have?" Katrina asked, opening her purse. "First round's on me."

Blair glanced up, "Oh, whatever's on offer. I'm easy."

Katrina ordered two lagers on tap, before propping herself up on the bar stool next to him.

"Sorry about Marcus," she began, taking a swig of her pint. "He has no filter."

"Oh no, don't apologise," Blair replied eagerly. "I don't mind people being honest with their opinions. It's the quickest way to learn the dynamics of the office."

Katrina simply smiled.

"How did your day end up?"

Blair adjusted his stool, trying to get it to the right height. "It certainly wasn't dull," he replied, "Dempsey is seemingly a good operator. Knows what he's doing."

Katrina chuckled before taking another sip of her beer. The noise around them grew louder as more people began to filter in.

"He's unpredictable, that's for sure."

"What did Marcus mean when he said to steer clear of Dempsey?"

Katrina dropped her shoulders, her eyes widening, "Jock's got some issues," she replied. "I don't know how much he told you about himself, but he used to work as an undercover operative for quite a while. Got himself tangled up in some big crime syndicate. Croatian's or Serbian's or something. It messed with him a bit. He's operation was terminated, and he came into homicide. I've only worked on his crew for a couple of years, but I've heard so many stories, which I'm sure have been exaggerated each time they've been told. Somewhere amongst them all is the truth."

"What sort of stories?"

Katrina tried not to speak too loudly, despite the sound of pool balls clinking behind her and an ever-growing crowd at the bar. She spotted Marcus entering the pub. It would only be a matter of time before they would be interrupted.

"From what I was told and take this as you will, he's job went south. Some say it was because he was at risk of being killed by some of the crooks within the group others say he was entangled in it that far that he had killed someone himself, to keep his cover. All I know, is that he prefers his own company and doesn't trust many people. I don't know if that's because he likes to bend the rules to suit himself, or just because he doesn't like the rest of us. What I do know, is that he's seemingly taken a liking to you."

"I wonder why?" Blair asked, sipping his beer and glaring at the ceiling.

"Fresh blood maybe? I don't know," Katrina added. "Enjoy it while it lasts. He doesn't have much to do with us but I can only imagine a bloke with his experience and knowledge would have a lot of war stories to learn from."

Within a matter of moments, Marcus was standing over them, waving a twenty-dollar note at the bar tender and ordering himself a beer.

"There you are!" he boomed, knowing full well that Blair and Katrina were seated right next to him. Standing alongside Marcus was another well-dressed, large framed man. He was more manicured than Marcus and seemed more relaxed.

"This is Henry," Marcus added, pointing to his offsider. "Also in our crew."

Before Blair could acknowledge his new work colleague, Marcus had reached across them all to grab his two beers from the bar.

"Tammy told us about those two missing women." Henry stated, taking his beer from Marcus and pulling up a stool next to Blair. "You guys looking into this?"

"Jock is," Blair replied smiling, "I just ride along and do what he says."

Marcus scoffed.

Katrina gave Henry a worrying look.

"You should come along with us tomorrow," Henry added. "We're heading out to pick up two crooks for some drive-by shootings in the eastern suburbs. Echo Taskforce is coming along. Would be good exposure for you."

Blair simply smiled and nodded. Seemed like a good idea, depending on Jock's thoughts.

"Have to wait and see what Dempsey says," he eventually said, putting his empty pot down on the bar.

"Fuck Dempsey," Marcus replied. The pint looked small in his enormous hands.

Henry put his hand on Marcus' shoulder, before responding, "Is that Silas Crowley you guys are looking at?"

"How did you know?" Blair quizzed, running the back of his hand along his lips.

"Jock was obsessed with this guy last time. He called in every favour he had to the OPP. He went out to Barwon Prison a few times and hassled Crowley even after he was convicted, demanding to know where the bodies were."

Blair could feel his face turning red. He could sense history repeating itself if today was anything to go by. He thought back to the home visit to Crowley's house and the private conversation that he wasn't privy too.

Perhaps it was history repeating itself.

"Thanks Henry," he replied, "I'll get the next round, but then I must get going. I have one more stop before I head home."

CHAPTER 9

BLAIR COULD SENSE DÉJÀ VU.

Different pub. Different atmosphere. The Elephant Castle. Two blocks away from the Bended Elbow.

The demographic of the pub had changed. This appeared more like a white-collar hang out. Where cocaine was snorted from the marble bench tops in the toilets and every second patron held a glass tumbler containing the finest whiskeys from around the world.

As he scanned the room, he'd found who he'd been looking for.

Dempsey.

Sitting at the bar with another male. He appeared the same age, black hair with streaks of grey. He was messy, his face shadowed by three-day growth and he wore a black jacket which highlighted his ageing features. It was as if life had chewed him up and spat him out.

Blair made his way over, moving through the crowd of suits and tapped Jock on the shoulder.

"You made it," Jock muttered, spinning around on his stool. It appeared that alcohol lightened him up. He couldn't imagine being greeted in such a pleasant way if Jock was sober.

His friend didn't look up from the bar.

"This is my oldest friend and finest copper I ever worked with, Zoran Kovac."

Zoran looked up and gave Blair a nod, before taking a sip of his scotch. No handshake. No greeting. Just the nod.

"Grab yourself a drink kid," Jock demanded, getting up. "While you're at it, I'll have a Scotch neat. I have to take a piss."

Blair reluctantly accepted the request, sitting in Jock's place as he made his way to the toilet.

"So, you're Chapman's kid?" Zoran murmured, still looking down at his glass.

"You knew my dad too then?"

Blair tried to make eye contact with the barman, who was busy telling a drunken patron off on the other side of the bar.

"John and I used to work with him. A long time ago now."

"You were in the job?"

"Twenty-five years," Zoran replied. "Most of it undercover, the last few years as a handler."

"Makes sense."

"What does?"

"I knew Jock was a U.C, I figured that's how you two knew each other."

Zoran grunted, taking another sip.

"What's your old man doing these days?"

"Golf. A lot of it," Blair replied, eventually gaining the attention of the barman and ordering Jock's drink, along with one for himself.

"He always was a shifty bastard," Zoran continued.

Before Blair could respond, he felt an arm reach through the gap between them and grab the vacant drink from the bar. Jock had returned.

"Ah fuck," he muttered, trying to balance his drink whilst

reaching into his pocket. He glanced down at the screen of his phone, "sorry boys, have to take this call. Be back in a minute."

The two of them watched on as Jock wandered out to the beer garden. Hoping to get some sort of silence to take his call.

"You know, he trusts you," Zoran continued. "He doesn't trust many people."

Blair took a sip of his whiskey, wondering why he ordered one. It was an acquired taste. Zoran didn't see him turn his nose up. His face twisting as he swallowed.

"He told you this?" Blair quizzed.

Zoran shook his head. "Doesn't have too. I can read Dempsey like a book. He doesn't get along with many people. He seems to like you. I don't know why, given what your old man did to us. I guess he figures just because you come from the same family, maybe you're not tainted by the same brush."

"What do you mean?" Blair eventually got the words out. "Dad's never said anything."

"He wouldn't," Zoran replied. "He cut our lunch. People who do that don't tend to acknowledge any wrongdoing."

"Is this about the Serbs?"

"Mafia. Serbian mafia. Led by a dude called Nikola Petrovic. We worked on this job for over two years. Had Petrovic and his henchmen on all sorts of charges from murder to drug trafficking to sex trafficking. I reckon we had about forty crooks lined up, including Petrovic."

"What happened?"

"Minister got word of our op. Shut it all down. Came from the chief right down to our superintendent. We had to pull Jock out. Give him a cover story. We both had to take extended leave. Someone leaked our details to the mob. The irony was that your old man took all our intel, our recordings, our statements, and made all the arrests with a new taskforce. Task force

Gemini. Only fifteen convictions, five of those copped sentences of ten or more years. Petrovic plead guilty, only did three years here and was extradited back to Serbia to serve out the rest and face the music with some crimes in his own homeland. Low and behold though, he made some bullshit deal with the government in Serbia, and he was out in less than a year of getting there. Got a pardon from the Serbian government. No doubt paid someone off. Very well-orchestrated."

"My Dad never told me any of this."

"What did he tell you?"

"He told me he worked on this task force, Gemini. The one you just mentioned. The arrests of the Serbian crime syndicate members and the court proceedings that followed. It's how he got promoted to Detective Inspector before he retired."

"Funny that," Zoran scoffed, taking a guzzle of his whiskey that made even Blair's toes curl.

There was a short pause before Blair peered up from his glass. "Why did the minister close down the job? Seems odd. They don't normally get involved in the groundwork, not to mention, how did he even know about it?"

"Command's cover story was that a couple of Nikola's men had turned up dead. They were alerted to it by some investigative journalists and when they snooped into our job, they realised Jock was involved. Which of course is a big red cross for any police operation. We both knew it was bullshit though, because the media don't just stumble on private police operations unless there is a leak. The real story is that the minister was on the payroll. The Serb's payroll. Once he knew or suspected something was going on, they knew, and we were all essentially fucked."

Blair exhaled. This was a lot to take in. No wonder Jock

was a bitter man. It was all making sense now. The hostility and the isolation. Any reasonable person would have trust issues.

"Why are you telling me this?" Blair asked.

"Why not? I don't give a fuck." Zoran added, finishing his drink. "I've done my time in the job. I've got nothing to hide. Whatever you want to know, just ask. But you won't get much out of the old boy. He doesn't talk about it."

"Tell me about Silas Crowley," Blair continued.

"Crowley was a means to an end. When you work on such a big job for a long time, and you dedicate your life to it and put everything on hold. Family. Friends. Hobbies. Lifestyle. Then it all gets whisked away from under you without warning or explanation, I guess you're left to pick up the pieces. Try to restore some sort of life for yourself. For Jock, it was about getting back into the action. Submerging himself in a task. A job. Something likely to have an outcome. For him, that was Crowley."

"I'm worried that its' more than just that. It's seemingly become an obsession."

Zoran laughed. "Yeah maybe. But that's Jock. He won't rest until his pinned the JFK assassination, Princess Diana's death, and Michael Jacksons overdose all on Crowley."

"It's not normal. Surely he isn't like this with every job."

Zoran raised his finger to order another drink, but the bartender ignored him, moving on to a blonde female waiting in the corner.

"Fuck head," Zoran muttered, before continuing, "Silas was Jock's link to the Serb's. You see, we suspected Nikola was involved in selling kids and young women to pedo rings. International rings. Big players. Jock could never prove it, nor did he have any leads. But he knew Silas was involved. Putting him in the slammer for a decade was Jock's way of closing the book. Not just on Silas and the missing kids. But on everything that had gone on for long before that."

It was making sense to Blair now, as he struggled to take another sip of his drink.

"Urgh," he murmured, putting the drink down on the bar. "So why would he be chasing him again now. After all these years. Quizzing him on these recent missing persons files?"

Zoran shrugged his shoulders. "Old habits die hard I guess. I've been out of the game too long now. I don't keep tabs on the old boy. That's your job now."

"But you're still mates?"

"We catch up once a month for a drink. But we don't discuss work."

"What do you discuss?" Blair asked abruptly.

Zoran scoffed and spun around in his chair, now face to face with Blair. "I've told you the back story. It's up to you now to work the rest out for yourself. Word of advice? Don't try and stop him. Just go along for the ride, cause it's going to happen with or without you. You might learn a thing or two."

With that, Zoran began fumbling around in his jacket pockets. "It was nice meeting you anyway," he continued, "you seem like less of a douche than your old man."

"Gee, thanks," Blair smiled.

"Next time you see him, make sure you give him this for me."

Zoran reached into his jeans and pulled out his hand. His fingers were all clenched except his middle finger which stood upright. The bird.

Blair laughed. "I'll be sure to pass on the message."

Zoran jingled his keys as he slipped on his jacket and disappeared into the sea of people milling around the pool table.

As Blair spun back in his stool to face the bar, he couldn't help but make sense of Zoran's story. Jock's past. Their relationship with his father. The fallout. The corruption. And Jock's ambition to make things right.

"You scare him off?" came a familiar voice from behind him.

"Apparently so," Blair replied, taking another sip of his whiskey. It didn't get easier. He raised his eyebrow and Jock could sense the discomfort in his body language.

"Stick to beer maybe?" Jock smirked, "leave this shit to the big boys."

Blair nodded. An admission of defeat.

"Bright and early tomorrow," he added. "Don't be late. We have a lot of work to do."

Jock finished his drink, slamming the empty glass down on the bar. He didn't speak another word, instead giving the bartender a wave and disappearing through the crowd to the rear car park.

Blair was left alone. Standing by the bar. The pub had gotten busier since he'd arrived. He glanced down at his watch.

9.15pm.

It was still early. Even if tomorrow was another workday.

"I'll have the same again," he said to the barman, reaching into his pocket for his last twenty-dollar note.

He'd started on the whiskey and figured it best to finish on it. Perhaps it was an acquired taste. If he was going to play with the big boys, he had to be like the big boys.

This was a start.

CHAPTER 10

"WHAT FUCKING TIME DO YOU CALL THIS?"

Blair raised his shoulders, wincing. Luckily, there was no one else around to hear it.

Jock stood by Blair's desk, holding a pile of folders. "If you're going to work in my crew, you need to be able to follow simple instructions. When I say seven o'clock start, I don't mean twenty past seven."

"Sorry," Blair muttered, lowering his backpack onto the floor by his chair, "I lost track of time."

Jock ignored his excuse, opening the folder and removing an image.

"Phoebe Davis," he began, sliding a photo of a young smiling girl across the desk so Blair could see. "Twelve years old. Went to her local park in Brunswick to meet some friends from school at 5.15pm last night. Never showed at the park. Never came home."

"How did you find this out?" Blair quizzed. He had sorted himself out and was now focused on Jock's folder.

"I got a call from a Sergeant at Brunswick uniform. They've done a thorough search of the area. Checked in with the family. Ran a check on the girl's phone, it's switched off."

"You think it's Silas?"

Jock didn't answer, instead closing the folder and returning it to his desk, where he rummaged through another pile of paperwork.

Blair unzipped his backpack and removed his drink bottle, taking a swig. He lowered the bottle back onto the desk and glanced back at Jock, catching the handle of a knife being slid into his police bag.

"You always carry knives in your kit?" Blair asked, smiling.

Jock again ignored him. "Read the file," he replied, "tell me about the link between Phoebe, Kylie and Sarah. I'll grab a car. Meet me in the car park in fifteen minutes."

Blair nodded.

"And one other thing—" Jock continued, "don't be late again."

Jock opened his police folder. It looked as old as he was. The edges were tattered and peeling. The cover had faded and the emblazed police logo on the front had lost its shine. But it was his original police-issue folder from his detective training days. Getting a new one wouldn't be the same.

"When did you last speak to her?"

Sandra Davis stood in her kitchen, waiting for the kettle to boil. She wiped her eyes with a handkerchief. Having two detectives sitting at her dining table was not the morning she had anticipated.

"When she left at about four-thirty last night," Sandra replied, leaning against a chair, "she said she was going to the park to meet a couple of her friends. Jasmine and Chloe I think.

They meet down there at least two or three times a week. We don't let her stray much further than that. Being twelve and all."

Blair took notes.

"Who else lives with you?" Jock quizzed.

"My husband and Phoebe's younger brother Chris. He's eight."

Speaking of her younger son made it even more emotional. Having to explain to him why he's older sister hadn't returned home.

"Any kids she's been having issues with?"

"No, not that we're aware of. She's a good kid."

Jock could feel the lump in the back of his throat.

"When did you first raise the alarm?"

"About six-thirty. She's never missed dinner, she's always home on time. When she didn't come home I knew something was wrong. Really wrong."

"What did you do?"

"I jumped in the car with my husband, we drove down to the park. There was no one there. I rang Chloe's mum and Chloe had told her they'd come down to meet Phoebe, but Phoebe had never showed up."

"What route does she take Mrs Davis?" Blair quizzed.

"It's only a ten minute walk from here. I can show you on the map if you like?"

Jock nodded. Both men made notes in their diaries as Sandra Davis opened her google maps app on her phone and guided them through the route in which Phoebe walked to the park and then home. It was nothing out of the ordinary. Mostly main roads and a couple of footpaths through open parkland.

"Have you retraced her steps?"

"We did." Sandra replied. "Then the police did it again last night. They didn't find anything. She had her phone with her. We haven't been able to find it, and it's switched off."

"What sort of phone does she own?" Blair asked.

"Just a cheap supermarket phone. One of those Samsung models."

Blair nodded, frantically scribbling in his diary.

"I'm going to ask you a very awful question Mrs Davis, but we need to know." Jock began, rubbing at his shoulder, "is there anyone that would want to hurt Phoebe? Or even you or your husband? Any family fallouts? Friendships that have gone sour? Threats of violence towards either of you?"

Sandra pulled a dining chair out from the under the table to sit down. The stress of the situation was becoming overwhelming and she struggled to stay on her feet.

"No." she replied in short. "We're boring people detective. Most of my family is in Adelaide and my husband only has his parents here. He's an only child. We both work shift work. There is no one I can think of."

"That's okay," Jock replied, "we're going to do everything we can to try and find Phoebe. If you receive a phone call at any stage in the coming days from a private number, be sure to answer it as it'll likely be one of us."

Sandra nodded, wiping her eyes.

The two men thanked Sandra for her time and wandered back to their waiting police car.

"Did general duties check for CCTV?" Blair asked, opening his door.

Jock closed his diary, zipping up the compendium. "Yep," he replied. "Two houses on the route to the park. Both show Phoebe on camera. Looks like she made it to the park, but whatever has happened there is a mystery. No cameras. No witnesses."

"Door knock?"

"Nothing."

Blair sighed, lowering his shoulders as he slumped back in his seat.

"What do you want to do now?"

Jock glanced across at his partner. "We need to catch this fucker in the act."

CHAPTER 11

"What are we doing here?" Blair quizzed, peering out of the passenger window.

Within the inner suburb of Fitzroy, Blair figured the home was too fancy to be that of a criminal.

"It's my place," Jock replied. "My daughter flies in tonight from Brisbane. I wrote her flight details down on a bit of paper inside."

"Why not just text her?"

"Because she's forever accusing me of not listening and forgetting things. I'd be proving her right if I have to ask again."

Blair laughed. "Father of the year, eh?"

"This is why she lives with her mother," Jock added. He got out of the car with Blair following close behind him. He wasn't going to let up this opportunity to see how his detective sergeant lived. You could learn a lot about someone by the state of their home.

"You guys separated?"

"Eight years now," Jock replied. "Divorced actually. I don't really want to go into it. But Lucy had the smarts to live with her mother. She comes to stay in between school and her social life."

Blair nodded acceptingly. He stood behind Jock as they entered together. Blair was immediately taken aback by the beautifully restored home. Polished floors and high ceilings, complemented by the modern, yet contemporary tone of the home.

"This is too neat and fancy to be a bachelor pad." Blair stated, taking in his surroundings as Jock wandered into the kitchen, rummaging through the paperwork on the bench.

"It's had the woman's touch," Jock continued, "My wife and I did all of this together. No way known would I be able to do this on my own."

Blair wandered into the living room, looking at the old photos on the wall. Jock in his academy days. Jock and his ex-wife on holidays on an island of some description. Jock with his ex-wife and two girls. They seemed happy. The girls were young. Maybe eight or nine years old. The photo looked like one of the theme parks in Queensland.

"Why did you split up?" Blair asked, interrupting the silence.

Jock reappeared in the doorway to the living room, holding a scrap piece of paper.

"You must have misheard me earlier," Jock replied. "When I said I didn't want to talk about it, it meant mind your own business."

Blair could feel his face flush. He misread Jock's cue earlier.

"Is your other daughter with your ex-wife too?" Blair quizzed, following Jock back to the front door.

Jock looked down at his watch. "We better get going," he

responded politely, "The inspector wanted to talk to us before she went home."

Detective Inspector Pauline Evans ran the Homicide Squad. Her office was a tribute to her career. Framed pictures of past successes, certificates and accolades.

Pauline loved her job. She was strong and confident. Her hair was shoulder length and neat. Her dress was a grey power suit. She had climbed to the top in a man's world. That said enough about her character and drive. At her age, this is where she'd likely see out her days. She had no desire to be promoted again. The Inspector was well known as the king of the shits and the shit of the kings. Meaning, she would sit on her royal throne when approached by her subordinates, but there were enough ranks above her to ensure her ego remained in check.

"Blair, how have you settled in?" she asked, taking a sip of her coffee and leaning back in her chair.

"Really good, thank you." Blair responded glancing around the room, admiring the accolades hanging on the wall.

"You wanted to talk?" Jock interjected the pleasantries.

Pauline turned her attention to Jock, smiling at him. It was kind and gentle. Blair sensed they had history. Perhaps colleagues for a long time. They addressed each other by first name, that was the first giveaway.

"Have you created an investigation shell for these missing girls?" The Inspector asked, sitting back upright in her chair.

"Not yet," Jock responded confidently, "been busy doing *actual* police work."

Pauline continued to smile. She didn't react to his sarcasm.

"Where are we at?"

"Sarah Stewart and Kylie Illevski. They were the first to be reported missing now about five days ago. The most recent is Phoebe Davis. There's no direct link to any of the girls. Sarah is, correction, was 18 years old. Went missing after a night out. No one has seen or heard from her since last Saturday night. Kylie Illevski is 20 years old and went missing in similar circumstances. Then it gets weird. Phoebe Davis is only 12. On her way to her local park, about a one kilometre from her house. We believe she made it to the park but suspect foul play after that. No one has seen or heard from her either. All the girls had mobile phones; all are switched off. The two older females had bank accounts, no activity on either of them. This is exactly the same as last time Pauline. The age gaps. All females."

"Do we suspect these three are linked to the same possible offender? There is a big age gap there." Pauline quizzed.

"I think they might be."

"Based on what evidence?"

"Call it intuition."

Pauline let out a single chuckle. "Your intuition gets you in trouble," she added.

"Two words for you," Jock continued, "Silas. Crowley."

Pauline's smiled had vanished, placing her mug gently down on the desk.

"For fuck's sake John," she began, "not again."

Blair smirked and put his hands behind his hand. His concerns around Jock chasing Crowley again were obviously shared by the detective inspector. Katrina and Marcus were right. Jock had an obsession.

"He's out of prison and look what happens. Within a matter of days. It's not a coincidence. We haven't had a reported missing person in inner Melbourne with this same pattern for a long time. This cockroach gets out of prison and we have three in less than a week."

Pauline crossed her arms, preparing herself to listen to Jock's reasoning.

"We need to throw everything at this guy." Jock continued, "but he's smart. Smarter than last time. We need to setup some surveillance on him, catch him in the act. Get on the front foot."

"I can ask a favour to the surveillance unit?" said Pauline. "But if they know it's for you, they'll shove it to the bottom of the pile. Maybe we put Blair's name to it? Give him some exposure."

"No," Jock interjected. "You need to speak to them. Tell them to fucking grow up and move on."

"You've burnt them too many times Dempsey," she retorted. "They won't do this job for us if they see your name on the application. It'll be excuses again, like last time. I suggest either we put Blair's name to this, or you ask your crew to help you and do it yourself."

Blair glanced across at Jock, just in time to see him roll his eyes.

"Is it worth doing a media release?" Pauline asked. "Warn the public. Get them being proactive. Make it harder for him. Perhaps he might slip up this way?"

"No, not yet." Jock replied, "I want him to think he's winning. He's on a power trip and he'll be puffing his chest out even more now knowing that he's out of prison and able to do this again."

Pauline's face turned to a frown as she leant forward, "You need to make sure you don't fuck this up. If Command gets wind of the fact that we made this connection and didn't get on the front foot, both our necks are on the chopping block."

"I don't trust command. Not after last time. The less people that know the better." Jock replied with a stern voice. He got up from his chair, opting to lean on it instead of sitting in it. "Give me four days. I'll nail this cockroach, then you can tell command how good you are and we all move on."

Pauline returned to her relaxed state as she dropped her shoulders. Blair could sense her entertaining his ideas.

"With all due respect," he interrupted, "I think the inspector's right Jock. The more help we have the better. It'll be easier to catch Crowley if we work as a team."

"Okay," Pauline replied, "four days John. Then I tell the superintendent what's happening, you create this investigation shell with all the information you have and we get the media involved."

Jock turned on his heels and wandered out of the office, returning to his desk. Leaving Blair alone with the inspector.

She took another sip of her coffee. "Trust him," she mumbled to Blair, "he'll get this done."

Blair nodded and thanked Pauline for her time before returning to the muster room, in time to see Jock swivel in his chair.

"You," he said pointing. "Outside. Now!"

Blair followed his detective sergeant down the hallway and out into the rear car park just in time to pass Marcus, Katrina and Henry returning to the office. Marcus was carrying a half-eaten steak sandwich with its oil oozing out of the paper bag.

"Hi Blair," Katrina greeted, raising a hand for a semi-wave as the three of them passed Jock without word.

Jock waited until they were gone.

"What the fuck was that stunt?" Jock muttered under his breath, turning to Blair.

"What do you mean?"

"Telling the detective inspector how I should run my investigation?"

"*OUR* investigation," Blair corrected him.

Jock's lips widened and his forehead creased. "Listen to me you insignificant little dickhead. I run this crew. I call the shots. This is MY investigation. You're a guest. You do what I say. If you're not happy with this arrangement, I'm more than happy to send you back to the suburbs to deal with domestic violence and shop thefts."

Blair peered down at his shoes, before returning his eyes to Jock. "I thought we were a team. Isn't that how this works?"

"Not in my crew it doesn't," Jock replied. He raised his index finger and prodded Blair in the middle of his chest, "YOU work for me. YOU do what I say. Am I clear?"

Blair nodded in silence. Refusing to make eye contact.

"Good. I'm glad we understand each other. Now get the fuck back inside. We have work to do."

CHAPTER 12

"Sorry I'm late," Jock muttered, hanging his coat off the back of his dining chair.

Penny sat upright, tilting her head back and accepting the kiss on the forehead from Jock.

"Have you ordered?" Jock asked.

"Not yet," Penny replied, "and just so we're clear, ten minutes is late. Thirty minutes is nearly being stood up. You're lucky I didn't leave."

Jock scoffed at her and smiled, "You wouldn't leave. You love me too much."

Penny relaxed and returned the smile, "Maybe you're right. But don't make a habit of it," she responded, taking a sip of her red wine.

Jock picked up a copy of the menu and scrolled up and down.

"I don't know why you're reading that; you're just going to order the steak like you always do." Penny added.

"Just making sure they haven't changed the menu."

She laughed at him. As he lowered the menu, he caught her eye. Penny was running her index finger around the rim of the wine glass, somewhat distracted.

"Do you just want to skip dinner and go back to my place?" Jock said, a widening grin on his face.

Penny kicked him under the table. "The cheek," she replied. "You make a time of seven o'clock, so I'm here at seven, then you turn up a half hour late with no apology and you have the cheek to just assume I'll succumb to a 'booty' call. You've got more front than Myer."

Jock lent forward on his elbows, "I'll make it worth your while?" he winked.

Penny shied away, smiling.

"You're not angry," he added dismissively, as the waiter approached with his tablet.

"The usual John?"

"Yes please."

"What about Jade?"

"This is Penny."

Jock went red.

"Sorry, Penny. My mistake. What would you like?"

"The seafood fettuccine please," Penny ordered, taking a sip of her wine. "Entrée size please."

The waiter tapped away at his screen silently before wandering away. Not another word spoken.

"Who's Jade?" she asked.

The shade of red moved from Jock's face down into his neck.

"Just a friend."

"A friend like me?"

"Jealous?"

"Don't tip toe around the question."

Jock filled his glass with water from the jug on the table.

"Just a friend Penny. I have many friends. Am I not allowed

to have dinner with other people?" Jock asked, dodging the question as best he could.

Penny rolled her eyes. "You're a jerk."

"I know. It's why you love me though. If I pay for dinner, will that make it up to you?" Jock asked, widening his eyes and tilting his head.

"You turned up late. So yes, that's two reasons now," Penny responded. "What does Jade normally order? She comes here often enough for the waiter to remember her name."

"She's my sister," Jock lied. It was the only way he knew he'd be able to get Penny off his back. As an investigative journalist, he knew she wouldn't let up.

"Oh," Penny slumped her shoulders. "In that case, you're off the hook."

"Thank goodness," Jock replied. "For a while there, I thought you were going to go through my phone and follow me home."

Penny let out a small chuckle.

"It crossed my mind," she added.

Jock moved on. "What's going on in your world? I haven't seen you for a couple of weeks?"

"Mark's got me doing some pretty shitty stories," Penny replied, "I did a piece two days ago about some new community rooftop garden opening near the Rialto. Riveting journalism."

"You take the good with the bad right?"

"Haven't had much good in a while. Turns out my usual source of information has gone dark on me of late."

Jock pointed his index finger into his own chest, "Hope that wasn't a dig at me?"

"Absolutely it was," she continued, "tell me you have something decent for me. I'll take anything."

"There is actually something," Jock said, lowering his voice. "Silas Crowley."

Penny's face dropped. "The kidnapper?"

"He got released from prison last week. Eight days out and we have three girls missing, including a twelve-year-old."

"Let me run something."

"Not yet. We're not going public."

"Are you serious? Is the police force gone crazy? You must!"

"I have bosses Penny. They don't want too yet. There's no reason to create mass hysteria and paranoia on some missing persons files, two suburbs apart with no link," Jock continued. "But I will call on you at some stage. I have a feeling something bad is brewing."

"Bigger than Silas?" Penny quizzed.

Jock waited for a couple walking past to sit down at their table before continuing.

"I had my suspicions that Silas was somehow linked to the Serbian's back when I was a UC. He was kidnapping young women, kids even. I'd heard whispers within the crime figures that the Serbs were playing around with sex trafficking, stretching out to the pedo rings around Melbourne and even internationally. But I could never prove it. Big money was being thrown around. Hundreds of thousands, if not million dollar price tags on girls. Being drugged and moved out to middle eastern countries. Nikola had people on his payroll with customs and border force. Easy to move people around on private flights."

"How did Silas fit into this?"

"Nikola never did any of his work himself. He always outsourced. No one internally did anything like this. I know because I was working within his inner circle. They never spoke about it, which meant the work was being done externally. Outside of his group. Meaning collateral damage was minimized. If anyone got picked up, there'd be no link to him or his men."

"Where is Nikola now though?" Penny asked, peering over her shoulder.

"No idea. He was released from prison in Serbia a few years ago. He could be anywhere. But if Silas is involved in this again, Nikola can't be far away."

"Can't you find out internally? If he's back, someone within the police force would have to be looking at him."

"I've tried," Jock stated. "We have nothing in our system. I've reached out to people at the federal police. They don't have anything active for him either."

Penny sat back in her chair. "What can I do?"

Jock shook his head. "Nothing right now. When the time is right, I'll reach out and give you what you need. For now, I need to dig a bit deeper."

"Who's working with you?"

Jock scoffed. "No one. I don't trust anyone. Not after last time."

Penny looked at him sympathetically, "you need to let that go Jock. Have trust in people. That was a long time ago. People change."

Jock wanted to tell her about the government officials he saw in the bar that night. He wanted to tell her the truth to what he knew. What he saw. But he couldn't trust her enough. It was too big a story for a journalist to simply resist printing, regardless of whatever relationship and trust he'd built with her.

"Chapman's kid has joined my crew," he replied, "Blair Chapman."

"As in, Daniel Chapman's kid?"

"Yep."

Penny sighed. "You thought he was involved somehow, didn't you?"

Jock lent back in his chair to allow the waiter to drop their plates of food in front of them. A different waiter this time.

"Thank you" Penny smiled, acknowledging her plate of fettucine.

Jock ordered a pint of beer before continuing, "I don't know. It was all so abrupt and I had nowhere to go to get answers. Even Pauline was kept in the dark. I was dragged out of the operation quicker than you could blink, and Chapman had swooped in and strategically arrested all the wrong people. Most of the big players were let go and Nikola was deported, which we knew was not going to end well in Serbia where corruption is rife. He did less than a year in a minimum-security prison before getting a pardon from some government official over there. It all reeked of corruption. It was as if it was all setup and planned from the get-go."

Penny's eyes lit up. "Let me dig into it. I can uncover things you can't."

"Like hell," Jock blurted, taking in a mouthful of food right as his drink arrived. "You don't know the half of it. More importantly, you don't understand what you'd be walking into."

"That's my job John. It's what I do."

"You call it a job," Jock continued, "I call it tugging on the tail of a venomous snake."

He watched as the color drained from her face. He couldn't make out whether it was disappointment that he wouldn't give her what she wanted, or whether she was legitimately scared of what she may get herself into.

"Hurry up and eat your dinner," he added, still chewing

his food. A sneaky grin emerged on his face, "then we can get out of here."

The morning sun beamed into Jock's bedroom, creeping its way in through the gaps in the blinds and hitting Penny in the face. It was just enough to wake her from her slumber.

She yawned and rolled over, reaching out for Jock but only finding that side of the bed was empty.

Sitting upright, she peered around the room and lent on her elbow, glaring down the hall.

Jock was nowhere to be seen. The house was eerily quiet.

That was until she heard the sound of whistling coming from the kitchen.

Penny slid herself out of bed and wrapped herself in one of Jock's old bathrobes, wandering out to the living room and then eventually into the kitchen. She half expected to find Jock making them both breakfast. The only absence was the smell of something cooking.

Except, it wasn't Jock. Instead, a young female. Maybe eighteen years old, she had ear pods in her ears and was dressed in activewear. It appeared as though she was loading whatever she could find into the blender.

"Oh, I'm sorry," Penny said, wrapping herself up tighter in the bathrobe, "I didn't mean to interrupt, I was just looking for John."

The girl smiled, peering across at her. "It's okay, I'm Lucy. John's daughter. Which one of my dad's friends must you be?"

There was a sense of sarcasm to her tone. Penny wasn't sure what to make of it, but she certainly knew the apple didn't fall far from the tree. With that attitude, Penny could confirm Lucy was definitely Jock's daughter.

"I'm Penelope. Penelope Acres."

Penny went to reach her hand out before realising she was on the other side of the kitchen bench.

"Nice to meet you Penelope," Lucy replied, an awkward smile on her face. "I think dad's gone to work. His car is gone."

Penny blushed. "That's okay," she responded, pretending she knew. "I'll just get dressed and let myself out."

Lucy gave her a courteous nod before peeling the banana in her hand and dropping it into the blender.

Penny made her way back to the bedroom, throwing herself on the bed. "Damn you Dempsey," she mumbled, "why do you do this?"

The Past

Jock looked up at the starry sky. The buzz of the city was now in the distance behind him and he found the quiet depths of the botanic gardens at night weren't creepy, but rather peaceful.

He'd seen everything in his line of work, so a stroll through the eerie park late at night was normal.

Jock glanced down at his watch. 1.10am.

He was late for the meeting, but it didn't matter. Chris wasn't going anywhere. Despite the time, there were still joggers and bike riders out. Hospitality workers cutting through the park to get home after work. Nightclub revellers using the route as a short cut to the next destination.

Jock made his way to the nearby park bench situated close

to a pond and small garden bed. Next to him was a dark figure, already seated. He was dressed in black trackpants and a thick hooded jumper, with the hood pulled up over his head. His fingers were trembling as he eased the cigarette from his mouth. The plume of nicotine escaped into the cool night sky.

"Why the fuck are we here Chris?" Jock asked, crossing his arms.

The figure released the cigarette smoke up to the sky. His left knee bouncing up and down. Nervous tension.

"I had to speak to you somewhere quiet, where no one would see us. I think Nikola suspects something, so I didn't want to draw any more attention to myself."

"This better be good, dragging me out here at one o'clock in the morning."

Chris nodded rapidly, taking another inhale of his cigarette before stomping on the remnants of the butt on the ground.

"Nikola has politicians in his corner," Chris began, sitting on his hands to keep them warm, whilst still bouncing his knees up and down.

"I know that Chris. Don't tell me that's the reason, this couldn't have been a phone call."

"It's not just that," Chris went on, "he has cops too."

Jock nodded, calmingly. Staring straight ahead. It was something he didn't know but kept the surprise to himself.

"I heard you were with Benny when they shot him. He was poking around in places he shouldn't have been."

"Why did he kill Benny?" Jock asked, turning himself around to face Chris.

"They were gunning for him. He was asking around about some young kids and something to do with paedophiles. He'd heard it through some low life drug dealer in Springvale. So,

Benny started asking Miroslav about it and Miroslav told George."

Jock gritted his teeth. "What did Benny find out?"

Chris shook his head and let out a nervous chuckle, "Fuck man, you gotta stop asking questions. It got Benny killed. You'll be next."

Jock stood up, ramming his index finger into Chris's forehead. The force edged Chris back against the park bench, he glanced up in shock.

"Don't fuck with me," Jock said sternly, through gritted teeth. "You bought me into this shitshow. Now you're going to tell me what you know, or I'll send you back to prison where you belong you little cockroach."

Chris's eyes were glazed, stunned. He was still tilted backward, attempting to keep his distance.

"Okay okay," he pleaded, raising his hands in front of his chest. "I didn't mean it like that. I just meant Nikola doesn't fuck around. If he finds out we've been talking, we're both fucked. No disrespect Mister Dempsey, but prison will be the least of my problems."

Jock grabbed a hold of Chris's shoulder and lurched him upright, grabbing at his pockets, first his hoodie, then frantically making his way down to his pants. Reaching into one side and removing Chris's mobile phone.

He turned on his heels and threw the phone. The sound of the water within the pond splashing on its impact.

"Now talk. No one can hear you and no one is listening. You can stop with this paranoia bullshit."

Chris's shoulders dropped and he sat back down deflated. Nikola had given him that phone. That was just another thing he'd have to worry about.

"All I know is they've moved into this sex trafficking

business. These last few weeks, all these girls have gone missing. Young girls, older girls, they cater for whatever the demand is. I don't know who is doing it and I don't know where they are going. But it's bad news. Some of these girls are just kids Mister Dempsey."

Jock lowered himself back down on the bench, sitting alongside Chris.

"Where did you hear this?"

The sweat was beading from Chris's forehead, despite the chill in the night air.

"Don't. Please." Chris insisted.

"I'm not going to ask again." Jock replied. His face flushed and the veins popping in his forehead.

Chris sat in silence for a short moment. It had served him right, bringing Jock into this business, in exchange for Jock turning a blind eye to drug trafficking charges. The trade-off didn't seem fair. Two or three years in prison, versus a Serbian mafia boss putting a bounty on his head.

"Benny told me. Three days before they killed him. He'd asked Miroslav because he heard a few of the boy's name drop one of the girls that had gone missing. Benny had heard about it on the news and put two and two together. He knew somehow that Nikola's group were responsible, but even Benny has boundaries. Kidnapping kids for a paedophile ring wasn't something he wanted to be a part of you know?"

The two of them sat in silence for a moment before Chris spoke again.

"I'm begging you Mister Dempsey. Don't' go sniffing around in this stuff. I know Nikola well enough to know he doesn't like it when his men veer outside their lane, if you know what I mean."

Jock smirked.

"You're a fucking genius, you know that Chris?"

"What? I'm just saying. I got you on the inside. You must be close now to ending this. Don't fuck it up by chasing shit that doesn't matter now. You'll be able to get all of them on the drugs stuff Mister Dempsey, you won't need to worry about the sex trafficking. That'll sort itself out."

Jock could see the logic. He gave Chris credit where it was due. He was semi-intelligent for a low-life criminal. He'd managed to stay out of trouble for this long, which gave Jock some relief.

"When you're so close to the end, why do you want to know about this stuff too? Aren't the drugs enough?"

Jock took a quick glance around him before replying. "Let's just say, I have a personal interest."

Chris nodded, standing up. "Be safe Mister Dempsey."

Jock gave Chris a sideways glance. He could see under the full moon and the look in Chris's eyes that he was terrified. Someone or something had gotten to him. Perhaps it was Benny's death or perhaps it was more. Maybe Chris knew more than he was letting on, but nonetheless, Jock trusted him. Chris had gotten him involved two years ago and had kept his secret for this long. Some criminals were meant to stay criminals. Others made some pathetic, half-arsed attempt at having some sort of a normal life. Chris was the latter.

Jock nodded at him, slid his black beanie out from his coat pocket and gently adjusted it onto his head, before walking off the way he had come. He recalled the first part of their conversation and what Chris had said, *'He has cops too'*.

Jock had known about the politicians. About the high rollers and those in the community with influence. But never had he suspected that police would be involved in Nikola's business.

If this was true, surely he'd be had by now? Everyone in

the organisation knew him. They knew who he was. His alias of 'Mick Murphy' would be dead and buried. But perhaps, they were playing him as he was playing them?

Now that he knew this, the game had changed. He'd have to watch his back.

CHAPTER 13

The Past

JOCK GLARED ACROSS THE TABLE AT ZORAN.

Zoran was normally a nervous wreck when confronted with superiors, but today, he didn't seem nervous. He seemed terrified.

His legs were bouncing around is if rocking a small child, with his fingers taking turns at being inserted in his mouth. His teeth trimming away at his nails.

Detective Senior Sergeant Danny Chapman sat alongside him; his glasses sat on the brim of his nose as he read through some paperwork he had spread out in front of him. Alongside him was Detective Senior Sergeant Shane "Robbo" Robinson and the only friend that Jock believed he had left, Detective Inspector Pauline Evans.

Jock had a sense he knew what was coming. He knew Pauline wouldn't be able to save his skin this time.

Before anyone spoke a word, the double doors to the conference room opened and Superintendent Bill Wright made his way into the room. He was tall and broad shouldered. He wore a dark blue suit, light blue shirt and a black tie hung from his neck. He had sharp black hair, neatly combed. Jock couldn't help but be drawn to the suit, wondering why he'd be wearing all blue, when all he had to do was put the uniform on. Sometimes old habits die hard.

As the superintendent sat down, it was Danny Chapman who spoke first.

"Thank you for joining us superintendent," he began, without raising his eyes from his paperwork. "We've called this meeting relatively quickly given the recent chain of events that have been bought to our attention involving the Serbian crime syndicate."

"Senior Sergeant Robinson has the latest updates from both Detective Sergeant John Dempsey and Detective Sergeant Zoran Kovac."

Danny Chapman glared across at his counterpart who then took his turn to speak.

Senior Sergeant Robinson cleared his throat, his glasses sat neatly on the brim of his nose as he read from the paperwork in front of him.

"Our analysts alerted us to a possible link around three days ago between this operation and a deceased male, Benjamin Miller, who was located in a dumpster in a rear alley way in Flemington. Yesterday, it was bought to our attention by other members working within the taskforce that another member of the syndicate's organisation, Chris Walker, who according to our notes, met with Detective Sergeant Dempsey two nights ago, has since been reported missing. Our intel suggests he's met with foul play. We've established there has been no activity on his mobile phone and his bank accounts have not been accessed."

Jock rubbed his face with his right hand. The news of Chris's death was news to him and he didn't know if he was more agitated at the fact that Zoran likely knew and didn't tell him, or that his meeting with Chris was what led to his eventual disappearance.

"Detective Sergeant Kovac has alerted us to the fact this operation has since uncovered suspicions around a human trafficking ring, one of which we previously had no knowledge of. This trafficking ring appears to be linked to a recent spate of missing persons reports involving children and young females in the local metropolitan Melbourne areas."

Before the Senior Sergeant could go on, Danny Chapman interjected.

"Superintendent, our issue is that whilst these detectives have worked hard and uncovered a new crime element involving this syndicate, the collateral damage that appears to be evolving as a result is seriously concerning."

The superintendent picked up his copy of the report, skimming through it whilst running his tongue along his teeth. He sat upright, with confidence. Spinning his pen around in his hand.

"Hmmm…" he continued, "I tend to agree with you detective senior sergeant," he began, looking up at Danny. "Any death that's occurred as a direct result of our interactions must be taken into account and considered. The fact that Miller and Walker both had interactions with Detective Sergeant Dempsey shortly before their deaths indicates more than just a coincidence. In saying that gentlemen, we need to be mindful of the cost of human life as a result of our direct interaction with this group."

Before Jock could speak, the superintendent continued, "not only that, but this operation appears to be fraught with danger, and there's no telling if our members will be next. Therefore, I think it's best we cease this operation effective immediately. Pass on all the intel gathered to Detective Senior

Sergeant Chapman's crew to perhaps begin making some arrests with the information we already have. After more than twelve months on this detective sergeant's, I can assume we have enough intelligence to start locking some of these criminals up?"

Jock shook his head, glancing at Pauline. She swung her chair around in the direction of the superintendent.

"Boss," she began, clearing her throat, "my only concern with ceasing this operation is that we've only just stumbled upon the beginning of this sex trafficking element of the syndicate. There is an opportunity here to further gain more intel around those involved and perhaps what's happened to these missing people. Particularly given some of the missing persons are children, no older than thirteen. This is concerning and we need to consider the opportunities in at least establishing where they've been taken and whether or not they are still alive."

The superintendent's face flushed. He didn't look at all impressed by the inspectors comments.

"I disagree Pauline," he added informally, dropping the paperwork back on the desk and leaning forward. "Two men have died thus far as a result of our involvement. If we begin making arrests, we're more likely to get some of these members of the syndicate to roll over if we make deals with them. I'd much prefer this method, as it's safer and we don't risk any more deaths."

"With all due respect sir," Jock interjected, "our involvement had nothing to do with those men being killed."

Jock expected somewhat of a significant backlash for speaking out of turn, but instead, the superintendent appeared to be calm. Possibly because he had the final say and therefore nothing Jock could say would sway him.

"Detective Dempsey, I'm not giving you this directive out of spite. I'm giving you this directive because I can see this ending in only two ways. They'll either be more deaths as a direct result of our involvement in this operation, or worse, they decide to turn on you. These two men have died immediately after your interactions with them. I've been in discussions around this with police command, who in turn have been liaising with the police minister. I can't see this ending any other way. We end this now and we start scooping these guys up. Is that clear?"

Jock glanced across the room, in time to see Danny Chapman's wry smirk evident on his face. The two made eye contact for a brief moment before the superintendent spoke again.

"I'll approve any funds needed to get you out and away from this mob. If you need to take an extended holiday, run it past the chain of command and we'll make it work. But you are not to return to this operation, nor are you to continue working with any contacts or sources. Am I clear?"

Jock leaned back on his chair, visibly annoyed. He nodded his head.

The superintendent got up from his chair and left the room briskly, leaving all the paperwork behind on the table.

"Thank you all," were his parting words as he closed the doors behind him.

Jock got up and followed. Zoran hot on his heels, leaving the brass sitting in the conference room to ponder the end of what had been a long and drawn-out operation. Without the result Jock had been hoping for.

As he entered the car park, Zoran stopped him, grabbing him by the shoulder.

"You knew this is how this was going to end Jock. As soon as they found out, they were always going to pull the plug."

"Bullshit," Jock replied, spinning around. His car keys hanging from his hand, "these pricks are corrupt. That's the only reason they are shutting down our operation. We're on the verge of exposing a massive sex trafficking and paedophile ring. Before, we only ever knew they were pushing drugs and guns. Now they want to end it all because two low-life shit bags are dead? That's horse shit and you know it. Did you hear what he said? The police minister knows. If he knows, then he also knows that we would have seen him in that nightclub. Snorting coke and fondling loose women. He wants to bury this entire thing and walk away. Chapman is going to be their ticket out of this. This will all blow over and all our work will be for nothing."

Zoran frowned. "You know the force doesn't like bad press and it certainly doesn't like bad outcomes. One leak to the media and it's a political shit storm. They'll blame us."

Jock shook his head, still unwillingly to accept Zoran's reasoning.

"Don't try and get me to see reason Zoran," Jock said, lowering his voice. "You've been by my side on this for over a year now and you want me to accept the fact that you are trying to see logic in their comments because Benny and Chris are dead? It's got nothing to do with them. It's the fact that people with authority now know that I'm on the inside and they don't want to risk it."

Zoran glanced down at the bitumen. Jock was right. Someone was covering their tracks and by closing their operation, they now had full control of the fate of the Serbian mafia.

"I've got your back Jock," he eventually said, his voice quiet and cracking. "I'm just worried. I'm worried you're not thinking straight and you're going a bull out of a gate with this. We need to be methodical. We need to have a plan on what happens next."

Jock rubbed the stubble on his chin, glancing at Zoran. He was deep in thought. Zoran was right. He's judgment had been clouded by trying to dig deeper into Nikola's new venture. He hadn't been thinking straight.

"I think I know what we can do," he said, a smile emerging on his face.

"What do you mean we?" Zoran quizzed, "you heard the super. We're done."

"It's been taken out of our control," Jock replied. "The rules of engagement just changed."

CHAPTER 14

The Past

THE TWO MEN SAT IN SILENCE FOR WHAT FELT LIKE an eternity.

On a cold Melbourne's night in mid-July, the temperature would have barely been five degrees. Zoran hated to think what the actual temperature was. He bought his cupped hands up to his lips and blew hot air in an attempt to stay warm.

As Jock began to doze in the driver's seat, the sensor lights from George's home lit up the night sky. In a suburban residential street in the middle of Kew, the two men sat in the darkness of Jock's undercover vehicle. The only light came from the full moon above and the bedroom lights of George's home.

Zoran glanced at the digital clock on the dashboard. 11.42pm.

As they sat in silence, Zoran slipped his black gloves on, stretching the material over his hands, then subsequently cracking his knuckles.

"Here we go," he said, nudging Jock and pointing toward the house. A large male figure emerged from the front door, dressed in black trackpants and a white t-shirt. He was barefoot, tall and of European appearance, holding a phone to his ear.

"Where's the medication?" Jock quizzed.

"In the glovebox," Zoran replied, sliding his beanie on.

"Remember, we come in from the east. We have coverage from that garden bed. When he wanders into the driveway, you jab him from behind and we'll drag him back the way we came in," Jock said firmly.

"No going back now," Zoran reiterated, grasping the syringe. "You sure you wanna do this?"

Jock turned to Zoran, the corners of his lips etched upward, his eyes lit up.

He didn't have to say anymore.

As George opened his eyes, he could see nothing but darkness.

He tried to move his arms but couldn't. He felt smothered. Tight.

Realising his face was covered, panic had set in. He wriggled his fingers. His arms pinned to his sides, with what felt like duct tape. It was tight against his skin.

Was this some sort of a sick joke? Were the bikies' out for revenge? How did they find him?

"Our friend is finally awake," a voice called. A familiar voice. One George knew all too well.

Mick.

"What are you playing at?" George bellowed, still trying to move his arms, attempting to break free. The tape pulling on his skin, making it worse.

Jock whisked off the face covering, and George glanced around. His pupils like dinner plates, trying to adjust to the interior lights. He was sitting inside a car. On the backseat. His arms bound by his sides. His ankles taped together. He sat on an angle, his body twisted, facing the inside of the car. Glancing outside was nothing but darkness. Bushland. They were far from the city now. The last he remembered was talking to Miroslav on his phone. Then he blacked out.

A vehicle parked ahead turned its headlights on, beaming the bright light directly into his car and directly into his eyes.

"What are you doing Mick?" he asked, again.

Jock approached the side door, opening it. He'd never seen George in such panic before. He seemed unsettled. Out of his comfort zone. Never had George been on the other end. Vulnerable. The power taken away from him.

"Probably need to come clean with you George," Jock began, leaning against the frame of the car. "My name isn't Mick. I don't work for you. Nor do I work for Nikola."

George smirked, lowering his head, "I knew it. I knew it from the start. You're a cop aren't you? I told Nikola I didn't trust you. I never did. But he always told me to shut my mouth. Told me I didn't know what I was talking about."

"Real shame," Jock continued, "you should have trusted your instincts."

"What the hell do you want?"

"I want some answers."

George let out a nervous chuckle, "You worked for us. You already know everything, what else is there you could possibly want to know?"

"The girls," Jock replied. His face remained frozen. Like the night air.

George smirked. "It was you asking around? All this time eh?"

Jock didn't respond, so George continued, "all this time I thought it was Benny. Then when we finished him off, Chris decided to start poking his nose around. Never did I think you were behind all the questions."

Jock interjected. "Well, now you know. So, time to start talking then."

"What makes you think I'm going to tell you anything? Where the fuck are we? Is this some shady police technique to make people talk? Kidnap them? What would your bosses say about this?"

"You would know," Jock replied. "You pay some of them, don't you?"

George held his smirk, "Damn straight. Funnily enough though, none of them told us about you."

"Looks as though you got played, hey George?" Jock continued.

George glanced up, still peering at the headlights ahead. "Sure, seems that way now that you mention it," he responded. "When Nikola finds out about this, boy oh boy…."

"That's the thing," Jock continued, "there's no guarantees in life. That includes you going home to tell your boyfriend about this."

George became silent. He had underestimated Mick. His weakness was not trusting his instincts. His instincts that told him that 'Mick' was going to be trouble. Now he was living his mistakes.

"Tell me about the girls," Jock asked again. He reached into his pocket, removing a pair of garden shears, unclipping the latch.

"You're familiar with this technique I do believe?" Jock asked sarcastically, waving the shears in front of George's face.

George glanced down. "If you're gonna kill me, what's the point in telling you?"

"I never said I was going to kill you," Jock responded. He

unhinged the clip on the shears, and showed them to him again, as he squeezed the handles back and forth, forcing the blades to retract. "There may be a little pain if you don't tell me what I want to know. That's always one good way to test someone's loyalty."

Jock could see the wave of panic rush over George's face. He could see the fear in his eyes.

"You can't do this," George said nervously, a quiver in his voice. "You're a cop. You're not allowed to do this shit."

Jock's eyes narrow.

"What strikes me George is when you remove the weapon from the warrior, that's when you truly know how the warrior will respond."

George swallowed.

Jock continued. "You seem to be happy to pull the trigger on command on an unarmed man, yet when you find yourself backed into a corner, with nowhere to go, you're nothing more than a coward."

"Untie me pig and we'll see how much of a coward I am," George responded, through gritted teeth. He thrashed his legs about in a pointless attempt at breaking free. The fear had now been replaced with anger.

"That's better," Jock replied. "Now, I'm only going to ask once more. Tell me about the girls."

"You fucking touch me and I'll rip your eyes out," George responded, attempting to move his arms again. The duct tape remained tightly in place.

Jock approached, lifting one of George's hands and separating it from the other. He held the garden shears to George's thumb, wrapping the blades tightly around the base where he squeezed the handles together.

The terrifying cries of pain echoed through the

surrounding trees. Closely followed by a stream of blood catching on the car seat. Pooling around him.

Jock picked up the end of George's thumb and held it to his face. "I'm not going to ask again."

"You mother fucker!" George screamed. "My thumb!"

"If I have to ask the same question ten times, you're going to run out of fingers."

"Okay," George muttered, breathing heavily through the pain. Jock could see his belly expanding with every frantic breath.

"The girls. They get sold onto the highest bidder. Sometimes locally, sometimes internationally. It all just depends."

"Who does the kidnapping?"

"I honestly don't know."

"Index finger is next."

"No no no!!" George screamed, "I'm telling you the truth. I don't know. Nikola's cousin, Mile. He arranges it all. They go to a secret location and they are held there until the bidders are sorted and the girls are sold. Once money is exchanged, they are moved from the location by different people. People that Nikola pays."

"Why have I never seen or heard of this Mile?"

"Nikola keeps this side of his business very quiet. It's private. People don't care about drugs and guns. They care when young girls go missing. That's why he keeps this part of the operation close to his chest. Only the people who need to know will know. It pays huge dollars. The girls fetch anywhere up to a million dollars. The last one went to somewhere in Saudi Arabia. I only know because I overheard Mile talking about it."

"Where do the police and politicians come into this?"

George shook his head. "Please. I can't tell you."

Jock approached the car again, hovering the blades over George's right index finger.

"Please no," George begged, tears streaming down his face. His brow sweating. "Please I can't. They will kill me. They'll know it was me. I'm fucked if I talk."

"You're fucked either way," Jock interjected, "I'll kill you myself if you don't tell me who these people are."

George shook his head. "You can cut off all my fingers. If I talk, I'm a dead man. They'll know it was me."

"Who?"

George shook his head again. Planting his head into the back of the front seat. He was defeated. For that split moment, Jock actually felt a sense of empathy for the man. Stripping back the bravado and the ego, George was no different to anyone else. It was simply Nikola feeding him power and he'd become drunk on it. Once that power was gone, the true George was exposed. The one sitting on the backseat of a car, bound and tortured for information. The tears and panic were real. The ego was gone.

Jock lowered the garden shears back into his pocket, leaving George slumped across the back seat. He wandered over toward the other vehicle where Zoran sat in the driver's seat. The headlights still lit up the fire track which led deep into the nearby bush.

"What did he tell you?" Zoran asked, his window down.

"Nikola's cousin, Mile or something, he arranges it all. Senior police and politicians are involved. He isn't saying."

"He isn't talking?" Zoran chuckled, amused by the thought.

"No. He's frightened. Terrified actually," Jock went on, "more terrified of them than us. They've got to him. He knows who they are, but he won't tell me. He's prepared to take any torture we're happy to throw at him. Including losing all his fingers."

"Fuck me," Zoran sighed, his shoulders slumped. "Well? Now what? He knows who you really are. You're screwed if we let him go."

Jock looked away, failing to respond. This made Zoran nervous. He was watched on as Jock opened the boot before returning with a jerry can. He marched back along the dirt track toward George and the other vehicle. Whenever Jock went silent, it made Zoran twitchy.

As Jock approached, he could still see the beads of sweat on George's face. Shock had set in. He sat silently on the backseat, his eyes closed, breathing through the pain. The wound still bleeding.

"I'll tell you everything," George mumbled, hearing Jock approach. "Whatever you want to know."

"Who kidnaps the girls?" Jock asked, lowering the jerry can.

"I don't know," George replied. "That I can't tell you because I actually don't know. Nikola doesn't tell me everything."

"Which police are working for you?"

George's silence was deafening. It was the same question, and the same response. Nothing.

Jock unclipped the lid for the jerry can, pouring its contents over the car and splashing it all over the upholstery.

"What the fuck are you doing?!" George pleaded, leaning back on the seat.

"Sorry George," Jock eventually spoke, "I was growing fond of you too. Despite our differences. I actually found your ego entertaining."

"Don't do this Mick. Or whatever the fuck your name is. Don't do it!"

George's cries had a heightened level of desperation in them. A dying man's last plea. Begging for his release. Begging for his life.

"Just let me go. I won't say anything. I swear!"

"You're right," Jock began, taking a cigarette lighter from his pocket and flicking it back to form a flame, "that part we can agree on. Where you're going, I know you won't say anything."

CHAPTER 15

Present Day

THE INSPECTOR WIPED AT HER BROW. FOR A COLD WINTER'S day, it sure was stifling in the media room at the Victoria Police Centre.

"Do you have any leads detective inspector?" One journalist asked.

"We are still working on these so I cannot disclose any information pertaining to our investigation at this time." Pauline replied. Textbook.

Another journalist cut in.

"Are you suggesting that we be more vigilant, especially with our children?"

The use of the word 'our' resonated with Pauline. The journalist had put a personal spin on her question.

"At this stage, we cannot confirm whether the incidents are related or not. So I don't want to speculate and cause unnecessary panic."

Penny cleared her throat before calling out over the rest of the media contingent.

"Detective Inspector, do you have any evidence to suggest Silas Crowley is responsible?"

The rest of the media pack went into silence. What did Penny know that they didn't.

The question caught Pauline off guard. She could feel her face flush and her neck turn a shade of pink.

"We have many leads, as I said, and we are investigating each one of them as we speak. That's all I can say at this time."

Pauline turned to Jock who was standing behind her with the media liaison officer, expecting a reaction, but he didn't seem bothered. Keeping his attention on his detective inspector.

"The inspector won't be taking any more questions at this time." A spokesperson for the media unit indicated, turning off the microphone.

Pauline stood down from the lectern and exited via the door in which she came.

Jock singled out Penny from the rest of the media fraternity, pulling her away from her colleagues who were still intrigued at how specific her question had been.

"What the fuck was that?" Jock whispered, grabbing at her arm and pulling her in close.

"Sorry," she responded, "but I wanted to get a bite, see what she said."

"Do you not believe me when I tell you that I am working on it and you'll know more when I do?" Jock quizzed, seemingly annoyed at her antics. "I'm sure I was speaking English when I said it. Don't take me for a ride Penny, I'll happily walk away from whatever this relationship is if you're going to abuse it."

Penny seemed embarrassed. Perhaps she'd stepped out of line this time but couldn't see past Jock's empty threat. She knew that he needed her as much as she needed him.

"You mean you won't sleep with me anymore?" she

responded sarcastically. "Then leave me to make small talk with your daughter in the morning when you disappear?"

Jock stood upright, letting go of her arm. He tugged at his cuff links.

"I would have thought you of all people would know that what we have runs deeper than a few cheap questions during a press conference," Jock continued looking back up at her, "I told you when I have more, you'll know. Don't pull a stunt like that again."

And with that, he turned on his heels and made a quick exit, following Pauline through the double doors and out into the hallway, leaving Penny to field more questions from her peers around how she came to have information about Silas Crowley.

Penny stood for a moment, watching her 'fling' disappear behind closed doors. Despite their on-again off-again relationship, she couldn't help but wonder who had the greater upper hand in all this. Was the source of information worth the heartache that came with the enigmatic John Dempsey. She would have to wait. Time would eventually tell.

The Past

Jock took another bite of his toast as he turned to page four of the newspaper. He was struggling to focus on the headlines as Olivia made a racket behind him, attempting to unload the dishwasher.

The sound of buzzing suddenly came to the forefront and

Jock peered down at his phone which sat on the table. It was Zoran.

"Morning," Jock muttered through a mouthful of vegemite toast.

"Have you seen the news this morning?" Zoran asked.

"I'm reading yesterdays."

"Turn on the television."

Jock stood up from the table and wrestled the remote from Lucy, before flicking it across to the morning news.

A journalist was front, and centre of the camera shot, behind him, a burnt-out vehicle with several detective's dressed in suits scouring around the shell of the car.

'A body has been retrieved from a burnt-out vehicle in the Macedon Ranges overnight. Police believe the passenger perished in a car fire in the early hours of this morning and at this stage are not ruling out foul play.'

Jock bought the phone back to his ear. "Was the fact that the body was bound how they deemed it foul play?" he joked.

"What do you want to do?" Zoran quizzed.

"Nothing. Let the investigation run its course. There's nothing we can do."

"No loose ends?"

Jock shook his head, before remembering he was on the phone. "No. See you in the office."

He hung the call up before sliding his phone back into his pocket, in time for Olivia to give Lucy the hurry up for school.

"What's going on there?" she asked, taking a glance at the television.

"No idea," Jock lied. "Some joker was found dead in his car this morning. Just thought maybe it was a crook that I knew."

He switched off the television, snatched his last piece of

toast off the plate before kissing his wife goodbye and fleeing out the door.

He had to get to the office and meet Zoran. Their next task was to focus on who this 'Mile' was and what he had to do with Nikola.

The Present

Detective Senior Sergeant Shane "Robbo" Robinson took the last mouthful of his meat pie, before dusting his hands. Crumbs from the pie falling all over the carpet in the muster room.

Jock looked him up and down, unable to recall his memories of his boss from a decade ago. A boss who was never this overweight and lazy.

"How do you want to play this?" Robbo asked, with a mouthful of food. Jock peering at the buttons on his shirt, expecting one to implode at any moment under the immense strain.

Blair, Katrina, Marcus and Henry all watched on from their seats. It was rare for their boss to get involved in investigations. He was either normally queuing at the bakery or eating at his desk. The only time he spoke to them was when he wanted something. He was long overdue for retirement, but the grossly large income ensured he would continue to come to work and do nothing rather than sit around at home.

The inspector stood at the back of the room and was the first to reply. Her arms were crossed, and she looked tired.

"I still think we need to get the surveillance unit involved. Follow Crowley around. See where he goes."

Henry gave a nod in agreement.

Jock stood up from his chair and wandered over to the whiteboard. The missing girls' names and their faces stuck to it with blue tac. Crowley's mug shot sat not too far away. In amongst the pictures were scribbles made by Jock. Leads. Camera locations. Actions already taken. It seemed bare. For good reason. This time around it was harder to establish the link.

"I've spoken to them directly," Jock said, aiming his response at the inspector.

"How did that go?" Marcus asked, sniggering. Katrina snorted. Henry simply glared at both of them.

"As expected," Jock replied, ignoring the sarcasm. "They're busy."

"What a surprise," Marcus responded, putting his hands on his head and leaning back in his chair.

"Does he have a car?" Katrina asked, her facial expression changing. "If he's our man, he needs to be getting around somehow."

Tammy approached from her desk, privy to the entire conversation. Papers in hand, she responded to Katrina's question. "A white Toyota van was seen in the area around the time Phoebe Davis was reported missing. We have it on two different cameras within reasonable distance to the park, but footage isn't good enough to get a registration. We believe it's a Toyota of some sort. Possibly a late 90's model. I've sent it over to our contact at Toyota to get a better idea."

Jock interjected. "Silas has no cars registered to him, nor does he store any at his home. Local CCTV around the area of his house have him coming and going from his property on foot. I suspect the van may be supplied by the Serbian's. I haven't ruled this out."

Marcus rolled his eyes. "You still on that? The Serbs were snatched up years ago. You got proof they've started up operations again in Melbourne? You know something we don't?"

Jock puffed out his chest. Anger burning in his belly.

"They never stopped and you'd be naïve to think that such a large running operation just shuts up shop and moves on."

Blair watched the two of them, like a game of tennis.

"Continue detective sergeant," Pauline interrupted, giving Marcus the evil eye.

"As I was saying," Jock continued, "my theory is we sit off his home and follow him. Get him to lead us to the van or better yet, something more incriminating. We split off into teams of three. Marcus you're with Katrina. Blair you're with me. Henry, you're going to escort Robbo. What we do know is there is generally a couple of days' which lapse between activities. Much like last time. Which would suggest tomorrow is going to be our ideal time. We intend on kicking off at around eleven-hundred hours and I'll provide more details then. Any questions?"

Marcus scoffed and rolled his eyes. Henry shook his head. There was silence from the rest of them.

Behind him, Jock's crew dispersed. Before Blair could get away, he felt a tug on his arm. It was Marcus, pulling him in. "Don't let that lunatic take you for a ride," Marcus whispered. "Be careful."

Blair nodded and watched as Marcus walked off, slapping Henry on the back and hounding him about the colour of his shirt.

Blair slumped down at his desk, before spinning around to face Jock. "Do you think this op tomorrow will work?"

Jock didn't look up from his screen. "I sure as hell hope so."

CHAPTER 16

Jock glanced at the digital display in his car. 9.15pm.

Another late night. It was starting to take a toll. He was tired and exhausted, realising that he wasn't young anymore and pulling these sorts of hours was a young man's game.

Leaving his kit in his car, he eased his way to the front door, but before he could get the key in the lock, the door opened. Lucy was standing in front of him, chewing down on an apple.

"Hello pet," Jock mumbled. "What are you doing?"

She smiled, "you've got company."

Jock shook his head. "Who?"

"You didn't tell me you had a girlfriend," Lucy continued, opening the door. "She's sitting in the living room. We've been chatting for the last hour."

Jock felt like a school kid that had been busted. This was where the parent-child relationship took a turn and now Jock felt embarrassed. "About time you moved on," Lucy smirked, winking at him.

"I'll chat to you later," Jock muttered, attempting to be serious as he headed into the living room. Sitting on the couch reading a book was Jade. She didn't see him coming. He didn't really fancy the company, yet he was torn. Was it rude to ask her to go home? He hadn't seen her for nearly a week.

"Hello there," she eventually said, peering up from her book. "Big day?"

"Uh-huh," Jock replied, dropping himself down on the couch next to her. He rested his hand on her leg, "what are you doing here?"

"I wanted to surprise you with dinner," she added, "I made spag bol and bought it over. Most of its gone now though, Lucy and I shared a wine and ate it."

"So, you've met Lucy then?"

"You have an amazing daughter. She clearly takes after her mother."

Jock smirked, nodding his head. That she did. He'll give her that one.

"I can warm up what's left for you?" Jade continued.

"I'm fine," Jock replied. "Not hungry."

He glanced across at Jade. He'd always had boundaries with women, particularly after Olivia left. He felt as though the women in his life had suffocated him. Home was now his space alone. It was his freedom. From work. From relationships.

"I didn't realise we were at that stage," he continued. "You know. the pop-in dinner stage."

Jade closed her book and put it down on the arm of the couch. She then crossed her legs and turned to face him. "You need to let someone in at some point in time," she replied. "You can't keep dictating terms. The people in your life are going to want more from you."

"Don't play your shrink games on me," he muttered, "I know all the tricks in your play book."

She loved that he could be so relaxed with her. Behind that cool and hard exterior was just another man who wanted to be loved. She could see it and she was praying that he would one day let her in.

"How about if I take you out for dinner then?"

"I'm absolutely cooked. Pardon the pun," Jock responded. "Think I'm just going to have a beer and call it a night."

"I'll have one too then," she replied. He could see the cheeky grin emerging on her face.

"Fine then."

Jock wandered into the kitchen, before returning shortly after, holding two beers by the neck of the bottle. He passed one to Jade, cracking open the top.

"How is work?" she asked, taking a sip.

"Work is work," he replied dismissively, "same old shit. I work in Homicide. That should pretty much paint a picture of how each day goes."

"Lucy said she saw you on the television. Standing behind your boss at the press conference on the news."

"Happens at least once a week. Lucy is never here, so it's a novelty for her." Jock replied. The cold beer was exactly what he needed. The cool liquid hitting his throat and giving him a deep sense of refreshment.

"What was your boss talking about?"

Jock lowered his beer, sitting it in his lap. "I've got a better idea," he continued, ignoring her question. "How about you tell me about your day?"

Jade smirked. "Ok then," she replied. Jock was clearly agitated with all the questions.

"I'm seeing a patient at the moment who is completely delusional."

Jock laughed. "You're a shrink. Isn't that most of your patients?"

"Actually, no." Jade responded, taking another sip of her

beer. "Most people I see display quite normal behaviours. Like you and me. They just need help dealing with isolated issues. Like anxiety or stress. I haven't seen behaviour like this in a while. It's like this guy is on another planet. It fascinates me."

"Who is he?"

"You know I can't say," she replied with a light chuckle. "Just like you can't tell me who you deal with."

Jock took another sip of his beer. She was right. He didn't argue the point.

Before Jade could continue, Lucy's face popped around the corner. "I'm off to bed."

Jock stood up from the couch, beer still in hand, "actually, I just wanted to have a chat to you before you go." He looked back at Jade, "if you don't mind of course?"

Jade shook her head, "not at all," she replied with an awkward grin, "I was just leaving anyway."

"Sorry," Jock added. He wasn't sorry. He'd convinced himself that the conversation and the company wasn't what he wanted. He wanted peace and quiet and time with his own thoughts.

"I'll call you later," said Jade, "it was nice to meet you Lucy."

Lucy lifted a hand and gave a gentle wave. "Nice to meet you too."

Jock waited until Jade had closed the front door.

"She's lovely," Lucy added, propping herself up on the stool by the kitchen bench.

"Yeah, she's okay," Jock replied, finishing his beer.

"You just need to stop being a dick," Lucy continued, "I also had the pleasure of meeting your 'other' woman yesterday too. I think her name was Penny?"

"Oh, for fuck sakes," Jock muttered under his breath, "it's not what you think."

"My dad being a gigolo? It's exactly what I think." Lucy said sarcastically. She was spinning on the stool, knowing that the conversation was making her dad uncomfortable.

"My private life doesn't have anything to do with you," Jock replied, attempting to assert his authority. "You just play nice and don't go blabbing to everyone."

"Your business, not mine," she replied. "I'm sure if I did the same thing you'd be annoyed."

"Did what?"

"Had two guys on the go at the same time?"

"When you become my dad, you can judge me."

"Well played," Lucy replied. "What did you want to talk to me about?"

"Crowley," Jock began, "he got released last week."

He watched the blood drain from Lucy's face. She stood frozen, unable to move. Speechless.

"How long are you down for? Staying with me that is."

She took a moment to compose herself before answering.

"I have Jen's birthday next week. I wanted to stay a bit longer so I could see her, but now I'm not so sure. Do you think I should go back to mum's?"

"You don't need to rush back to Queensland. It's not the same as last time, you don't have anything to worry about."

"So why would you tell me?"

"I didn't want you to find out from someone else and then tell me off because I didn't tell you."

"Oh my god." Lucy had a sudden revelation, her eyes widening. "Is he the reason you were on television? Is he responsible for that little girl going missing?"

"We don't know yet," Jock said, resting his hand on her shoulder. "Don't panic and don't worry. I'm going to take care of it like I did last time."

"It didn't work last time. Look at what happened."

Jock stood back, exhaling loudly. Lucy was right.

"You'll just need to have faith and trust me," Jock continued, "when I tell you I'm going to take care of it."

Lucy nodded, tears welling in her eyes. The emotion she'd been holding back had now surfaced. The whole idea of Silas Crowley free to roam, to pick up where he left off was now weighing on her. She couldn't shake the thought of it in her head.

Jock approached her, reaching out and putting his arms around his daughter. Bringing her in close.

"It's okay Luce," he whispered, "you have nothing to worry about. I want you to stay as long as you want."

She looked up at him, wiping away the tears from her cheek. "Thanks," she whispered.

He let her go and watched on as she wandered out of the kitchen and out of sight down the hall.

Jock returned to the living room, slumping himself down on the couch. Not the homecoming he'd been expecting. Living alone generally meant peace and quiet when he'd come home after a long and tedious day. Whilst having Lucy visit was a nice change, coming home to see Jade bought back memories of married life and the chaotic nature of the verbal arguments and constant disagreements. It was his lasting memory of Olivia before she left. The noise of the television going; of the oven and rangehood blasting and the aromas of dinner wafting around the house. It was a stark contrasting difference to live now. All of that was gone. It was just him and his thoughts.

He took another sip of his beer. Chatting to Lucy had meant his drink had lost its crisp cool edge. He winced whilst gulping it down. It was now warm. Disgusting.

Jock wriggled in his seat, his equipment belt still on and

digging into his hip. He sat in silence for a moment before unclipping his holster and sliding back his firearm, bringing it up onto his lap and running his hand over the cool feeling of the metal barrel and plastic grip.

He picked it up and gripped it in his right hand. Pointing it at the television, closing one eye, he lined up the sights on the blank screen. Then twisting his wrist and lowering his elbow, he bought it to his chin.

He closed his eyes and thought back to his previous life. One that he hadn't destroyed. One that he hadn't let his work over run and drive all of those people away from his life that he loved most.

Jock thought of Olivia. Of her new life in Queensland with her new husband. She wouldn't have gone if he hadn't of let his job consume him. Jock thought of Lucy. Thought of what she'd do if he wasn't here. Continuing with life and doing great things. They didn't need him. Nobody did. Jade and Penny were nothing more than flings. Friends with benefits. He couldn't see a future with either of them. Having them around was fun, but nothing more. The thought of having someone move in again with him was repulsive. He preferred the quiet. He preferred being alone. Jock knew it was his own way of punishing himself for his sins and taking for granted the family he once had. He didn't deserve to have them. He'd blown what he had and got what he deserved.

Jock could feel the cold touch of the metal barrel pressing against his chin. Is this how they did it? Perhaps through the temple would be more accurate?

Then the thought of Lucy popped into his mind again. She would be the one to find him. To hear the gunshot and come running.

He couldn't do that to her. Whilst it would be a bittersweet end for him, the thought of putting her through such a horrific experience terrified him. Finding her father on the couch, his brains splattered across the wall was a sight nobody should ever have to see, let alone his own daughter.

The sense of emotion become too much. It was overwhelming. He could feel his eyes welling with tears. As he lowered the firearm, he heard footsteps in the kitchen.

Lucy had returned.

He quickly slid the gun back into the holster. The sound of it clipping into place drew attention to him, as Lucy stuck her head around the corner. Not expecting him to still be there, her pupils were dilated, attempting to adjust to the darkness of the room in which he sat.

"What are you doing sitting here in the dark?" she quizzed.

He skulled the last of his warm beer, lifting himself up from the couch. "Just working out my plan of attack for tomorrow," he lied, leaving his empty stubby on the kitchen bench.

As he wandered from the kitchen, he felt an enormous tug on his shirt, followed by a bear hug. He glanced down to see Lucy's arms wrapped around him; her head resting on his back.

"Love you dad."

He ran his fingers over her intertwined hands on his chest.

"Love you too Luce."

CHAPTER 17

The Present

8.07am.

MARCUS LENT ACROSS AND TURNED THE HEATER down, much to Katrina's dismay. Their unmarked police car sat parked two streets away from Silas Crowley's home.

"Are you crazy? It's like four degrees outside!"

He gave her a dismissive laugh. "Put another coat on then, I'm roasting."

"So? Crack your window or take your shirt off."

"You'd like that wouldn't you?" he winked at her.

Katrina scoffed at the thought.

"I don't even know what we're doing here," he began, "this is what the surveillance unit is for. This isn't our job."

Katrina smirked, turning the heater back on. "Surveillance unit said no remember? That's why we're stuck doing this."

"It's like déjà vu, doing this shit again. I can't believe he got Crowley locked up last time," Marcus replied in disgust. "He needs to retire already. What is he? Sixty?"

"I don't think he's that old," Katrina replied, running her hands along the steering wheel. "And you know what?

Sometimes it's the devil you know. He leaves us alone, unless on the rare occasion he needs our help. He doesn't micromanage, hell, he doesn't even check our paperwork properly. He doesn't toe the corporate line. If he goes or retires, they'll replace him with some squeezer who'll want everything done by the book. You need to let it go already. Move on Marcus."

Marcus adjusted his seat so he could lay back, slipping his hands on his head. "I'd take Putin over him. There! I said it. I'd trust a Russian dictator before I trusted Dempsey."

"Bit extreme!" Katrina squawked, "he's not that bad."

"Were you born yesterday? Haven't you heard the stories?"

"What stories?"

"He used to take money from crooks. Bribes. The old 'brown paper bag' shit."

"As if!"

"Serious!" Marcus replied, getting animated. "He worked an undercover operation for two years and made a mess of it. Another crew had to come in after him and make all the arrests. His intel and evidence was so poor, they couldn't convict half the crooks."

"Where do you hear this shit?" Katrina asked, laughing at him.

"Never you mind, I have sources," he replied, laughing back at her.

"The only source you've ever had is of the tomato variety. Maybe barbeque."

"You're a funny fucker aren't you?" Marcus replied, peering out the window.

The sound of the radio in the background put a stop their banter. It was the detective senior sergeant.

'Robbo here' came a voice on the other end, *'is everyone where they need to be?'*

"Eagle One in position," Marcus said into the radio sarcastically.

Katrina shook her head. "Do you take anything seriously?"

The silence from the other end was deafening.

"You see," Katrina continued, snatching the radio from him, "the boss is probably scratching his head right now wondering what the hell you are on about."

"Pfft" Marcus scoffed, "Robbo is probably face deep in an apricot Danish as we speak."

Katrina pressed the button on the radio, "Marcus and I are on Grey Street. We have obs on Crowley's usual route from his home."

"Thanks Katrina," came the response.

"Squeezer," Marcus muttered.

There was a short moment of silence before another voice was heard on the radio. This time, it was Jock.

"Katrina, can you and Marcus please move out to Lygon Street. Henry is going to be on foot, and I don't want to risk spooking Crowley."

Marcus shook his head, remaining silent.

"Sure thing." She replied, starting the car.

"He has no idea what he's doing. Makes it up as he goes along." Marcus eventually spoke, adjusting his seat back upright.

As their car pulled away, Henry approached on foot. A thick black coat covered his equipment, and his torn jeans and brown boots made him appear as a civilian. He reached into his pocket and retrieved a beanie, slipping it over his head.

At the other end of the street, Jock and Blair sat in a small hire car.

"He knows both of us," Blair muttered, "do you want to move further back?"

Jock glanced across at him. "How many times do I need to put you back in your box?"

"Sorry!" Blair replied, raising his hands in the air, "just a suggestion."

"Keep them to yourself."

"Righto."

The two men sat in silence for the next hour. Watching on as Henry paced up and down the street, sitting down at a nearby bus stop. Attempting to be somewhat discreet.

They watched on as people came and went. Mothers with prams taking their kids for a morning stroll. The elderly getting out for their daily exercise, some of them in groups. The occasional local with mental health issues, screaming at himself before disappearing back into whichever home he'd came out of.

It was close to ten o'clock before Silas Crowley emerged from his home, his hands deep in his jeans pockets as he wandered down his street heading away from Jock and Blair.

They watched on as Henry followed, keeping distance.

Jock got out of the car. "Get out," he said to Blair.

Blair unclipped his seatbelt and opened his door.

"I want you to follow Henry. But keep your distance and always have Henry in view, in case shit goes sideways."

"What are you going to do?"

"I'm getting out on foot."

Blair shook his head. "You're determined to blow this aren't you?"

"Kid, what have I told you? Mind your own business and do what you're told."

Blair snatched the keys from Jock's hands and slumped into the driver's seat, slamming the door.

"Fuck me," Jock muttered under his breath. He slid a pair

of black gloves on and adjusted his New York Yankees baseball cap, before wandering off from the car.

He watched on as Blair slowly accelerated away, following Henry down the road.

Jock waited until they were all out of sight, edging his way to Silas' home before wandering up the driveway and approaching the side fence. Sliding his hand into the hole in the fence, he unhooked the latch, opening the gate and making his way down the side of the house.

He peered over his shoulder, ensuring no one had followed him, before eventually getting around to the back of the house. The backdoor comprised of a flimsy security screen covering a thin wooden door with an older style handle that simply pulled down.

Jock opened the security door before jiggling the handle. It was unlocked.

He slowly opened the door, edging his way inside. The backdoor opened up into a small laundry which was attached to the kitchen.

Jock eased his way into the kitchen. Peering around at his surroundings, it was evident that Silas lived a somewhat empty life. The house was neat and tidy. There were no photos or pictures on the walls, nor anything to suggest he had anyone else in his life. He was a loner, that much was evident.

As he made his way from the kitchen into the hallway, his radio began emitting sound from his coat pocket, startling him.

"For fuck's sake," he whispered to himself, reaching into his overcoat and adjusting the volume, in time to hear the tail end of Henry mumbling something over the airwaves.

"Can you repeat Henry?" he asked, holding the radio up to his face.

There was an initial silence before Katrina spoke. "Henry

can't talk," she began, "he just said that Crowley is getting on the number 27 bus. We're just working out now where it's heading."

"Roger," Jock replied.

He clipped the radio onto the back of his pants before continuing down the hallway. With Silas out and about, he had all the time in the world. Making his way into the first bedroom, he rummaged through the cupboard, the bedside drawers and peered under the bed. Nothing but clothing and boxes containing photo albums, old magazines and books. It was hardly the bedroom of a notorious criminal.

Jock wandered back out into the living room. Peering around, there was nothing, but a television mounted on an entertainment unit and a three-seater couch with a small coffee table off to the side. The remainder of the room was immaculate. No photographs. No clutter. Nothing personal about it.

There had to be something in the house that incriminated Silas Crowley. Something Jock could use. He peered around the home but struggled to find anything out of place. This wasn't the home of a sadistic kidnapper and potential killer. Half expecting to at least find rope, tape, possibly even gloves. Instead, there was nothing.

Jock wandered over to the window in the nearby dining room that overlooked the backyard. Moving the blinds back, there wasn't even a garden shed. Nowhere to keep tools or implements that would help Silas commit his crimes.

Perhaps Crowley had another location? Perhaps he wanted to distance his sick hobby from his real life. As Jock walked back into the living room, he clipped the edge of the rug, lifting it up from the hardwood floors below. Glancing down, Jock noticed a small notch missing from the timber panel, wide enough to fit a hand through. As he got down on his hands and knees,

Jock pulled the rug back, exposing a wider section of the floor, except this time, there was a square outline of a cut in the timber. As he slipped his hand into the notch, he forced up the wooden floorboards, lifting a small panel away and exposing a short set of stairs that led down into the darkness of the abyss below the house. Jock had found some sort of underground bunker attached to the house.

'Bingo,' he whispered to himself in excitement. This was the rainbow unicorn he'd been trying to find all this time. As he fumbled around for his torch, Jock pointed the light in the direction of the stairs. Four short steps that led down into a narrow opening. It was just wide enough for him to stand in the confined space. In any other home, this could easily be mistaken for a modified wine cellar, but Jock knew this was no ordinary home. This belonged to a crazed lunatic. He took the short stride down the steps and into the bunker. The flooring and walls were dirt and the area around was empty. Jock shone his torch around; he was looking for something. Anything.

Just as the light of his torch hit the far corner of the bunker, he'd found what he'd come looking for. There, semi submerged in the loose dirt was a clump of brown hair.

CHAPTER 18

Jock had found what he'd come for. It was something proving his point all along that Silas was likely responsible for the three missing girls since his prison release. All he needed now was to prove this belonged to either one of them. Finding the hair was only the beginning. He'd have to work backwards now to somehow find circumstantial evidence that would get him a warrant, then he could come back and search the home where he would find the hair. A second time.

Jock closed the bunker and returned the rug to its usual spot. He knew he had Silas by the balls.

Finally.

He slipped the hair into a plastic evidence bag to not contaminate it. He knew he wouldn't be able to test it until he found it 'officially'. It made him realise, if there was hair in this bunker, there surely had to be something else in the home.

Jock returned to Silas bedroom and turned it upside down. As he opened the drawers, he tipped their contents onto the bed. It was clear that Silas had a fetish for women. Most of the magazines were either Playboy or Penthouse, or old lingerie catalogues. In amongst them, Jock found a white envelope, which was unsealed. Opening it up, he realised it was filled with cash. One-hundred-dollar notes. Crisp and green, there would have to have been at least five thousand dollars in there.

Jock shook his head. This money had to be payment for nabbing these girls. Where else would Silas have gotten such cash? He pulled it out from the envelope, folding it in half and slipping it into his coat pocket. *'Fuck him'* he thought, Silas wasn't keeping this. As he continued to rummage through the remainder of the drawers, the sound of his phone ringing broke the silence startling him.

It was Katrina.

"What is it?" Jock asked abruptly. His heart was still beating out of his chest.

There was a pause at the other end before Katrina eventually spoke.

"It's Silas," she began, "he's made us."

"What are you talking about? You're in civvies and he's never met you."

Another short pause, before she spoke again.

"He's sitting on a park bench outside Fitzroy Primary."

Jock knew he had Silas this time. Having been convicted of the kidnapping of a minor all those years ago, Silas had been placed on a court order upon his release. He was not to be within a hundred metres of a school.

"Did you arrest him?"

"We didn't have too," she continued, "He approached Henry and introduced himself. Then told Henry to take him in so he could speak with you."

"Can I sit in on the interview?" Blair asked, sitting down at his desk.

Jock brushed him off. "I'm taking Henry in with me. He's met you, so he'll play on that."

"Righto," Blair replied, trying to hide his disappointment. "What's the plan?"

"I'll fill you in when we're done." Jock replied abruptly.

As Jock rummaged through his kit bag, trying to find his folder, the wooden handle of a knife propped up, protruding from the bag. Blair caught a glimpse of it before Jock tucked it away again.

"You always carry kitchen knives in your kit?" he asked.

Jock flipped the top of his bag over before zipping it up.

"If you've nothing better to do, I can find some work for you? There's a mountain of property entries that need to be audited."

Blair swung around in his chair, returning to face his computer. "I'll give that a miss."

"Where did you go anyway?" Blair asked, typing away at his keyboard, trying to log back into the system, "when we followed Crowley. Where did you get too?"

"I scouted around his house," Jock replied, walking away from Blair to avoid any further interrogation.

Jock approached Tammy's desk, retrieving the plastic evidence bag from his pocket and sliding it out in front of her. "Can you enter this into the system?" he asked her, "I found it outside Crowley's house. I want to get forensics to see if they can get a DNA hit on it."

Tammy nodded. "Good get," she replied. "What are you expecting to come from it?"

"I don't know," Jock replied, "could belong to anyone. But it's a start."

What Tammy didn't know is Jock had separated the hair follicles. Retaining half of them in his bag to keep for later to plant back in Crowley's home. It wasn't a fool proof plan, but it was something. Hopefully it would pay off. He didn't have a warrant to enter Silas home, therefore, he had to make sure the evidence would still be available for later, when he would eventually get one and complete his search 'by the book'.

"I'll be in the interview room if you need me," Jock continued, picking up his police folder and disappearing down the hallway.

Blair stood up and wandered over to Tammy. "Why do I get the feeling he's up to no good? Is it just me?" Blair asked her, keeping his voice low.

Tammy laughed, taking a slurp from her can of coke. "That's Dempsey for you," she replied. "He does his own thing and it's best if we don't ask questions. You'll soon figure it out."

Blair lowered his shoulders. "That's what I'm worried about."

CHAPTER 19

Henry Cromwell was relatively new to the Homicide Squad. With no wife and no children, the hours and manic lifestyle didn't bother him. He loved his job. It was probably why he hadn't formed his own opinions yet of his detective sergeant. Henry saw only small portions of what the others did, but he always preferred to see the best in people and keep his opinions to himself. On some level, Jock knew this, and it was why they worked well together. They did not encroach on each other's space and there was a mutual respect between them.

He glanced up at the fluorescent lights of the interview room. They seemed dimmer than usual. It was certainly better than making eye contact with Silas Crowley sitting opposite him.

"Will Sergeant Dempsey be long?" Silas asked.

Henry looked down from the ceiling, in time to catch Silas wide smirk. Exposing his yellow stained teeth and greasy long black hair.

"Can you read me my caution and rights again?"

Henry shook his head. "No need too. The detective sergeant will do all that in the interview."

The grin remained on his face. Silas kept his gaze on Henry. There was a sense of discomfort. Henry refused to play into his hands, instead, opting to stare at anything else.

Outside the interview room, Jock and Katrina watched on from behind the one-way screen.

"He's creepier than I remember," she muttered. "There's just something about him."

"Tell me again what happened after I left you." Jock asked.

She brushed the hair away from her face. "He got on the bus when we last spoke and Henry followed him. The bus took him to Fitzroy, to George Street. We followed the bus in our cars and when Silas got off, he walked straight to the local primary school. Then he approached Henry and introduced himself, and asked if you could come and get him. He plonked himself down on a park bench outside the school and just watched the kids play while we spoke to you."

Jock shook his head.

"It's as if he knew we were following him, yet I don't know how. Henry wasn't carrying any kit. Then he breached he's order by going near the school, essentially forcing our hand to arrest him. He's risking going back inside the bin. All to just talk to you."

Jock stood back and continued to watch Crowley through the glass. How he was seated, how he was interacting with Henry. He's weird stare and inability to blink.

"I don't want to interview him."

"What?" Katrina asked, surprised.

"This is what he wants. I don't want to give him what he wants. I want to see how he reacts. I want you to go in there and start the interview."

"What the hell do I say?"

"You're a detective aren't you?" Jock replied sarcastically.

"He's breached his prohibition order. It's not fucking rocket science. Or do you want me to ask the junior Chapman?"

"No no, I'll do it." She responded, swallowing hard.

"Put whatever thoughts are going through your mind aside," Jock added. "He's a registered sex offender who is in breach of his order. That's it. Forget about his behaviour. You have a job to do."

Katrina nodded. The pep-talk had put her self-doubt at bay. After all, Crowley was just another crook through the revolving doors. Nothing more.

She left Jock standing by the glass and wandered into the room, lowering a plastic binded folder on the desk.

Crowley stood up, greeting her with a smile and a nod, before sitting down as she pulled her chair in. He'd turned his attention purely to her, now ignoring Henry.

"No Dempsey?" he asked.

Katrina peered up at him from her folder. He was grotesque. Between his long black oily hair and facial stubble, Crowley appeared as washed out as an 80's rock star after a three week cocaine bender. Without the rugged sex appeal.

"He's a bit busy at the moment," Katrina replied, opening the folder and flicking through the plastic pockets.

"You must be Katrina?"

"You guessed right." Katrina replied, the frown was evident on her face, unsure of how Crowley knew her by first name.

"I'll take it by the expression on your face, you're wondering how I knew?"

She smiled back at him. "Not really," she added, "my name isn't important. What's important is why you are here."

"Do I frighten you Katrina?" he asked, leaning forward on the desk, and propping his elbows up, "if I do, I certainly don't mean too."

Henry sat back in his chair, interjecting. "Let's get this interview going shall we?"

"Are you the bad cop Henry?" Crowley asked, slowly turning his head. "Is Katrina good cop and you're bad cop? Is that how this is going to go?"

He continued to stare. Both hands planted firmly on the table, leaning in.

Before Katrina could reach across to turn the recorder on, there came a short knock on the door before it opened.

It was Jock.

"Here he is!" Crowley stated, leaning back in his seat, interlacing his fingers behind his head, "I was wondering when you'd come and say hello."

"I'll do this," Jock mumbled to Katrina, taking the folder from her. "You can sit this one out."

"You sure?" she whispered.

Jock nodded. Having Katrina in the room would be a distraction to Silas. Someone new to antagonise and bait and Jock couldn't have that.

Katrina passed over the folder and exited the room, closing the door behind her.

"You've kept us waiting Mister Dempsey," Silas continued, "Henry and I have nothing left to talk about."

"Sorry to keep you waiting Silas," Jock replied, resting his hand on the folder.

"Could I see what's in that folder?" Silas asked, still smiling widely.

Jock started the digital video machine, going through the usual preamble, caution and rights.

Crowley straightened himself up in the chair and closed his eyes. His lungs expanding and contracting slowly. Breathing deeply.

"Can you tell me why you're here?" Jock asked, commencing his line of questions.

Silas paused, glaring at Jock, before turning his attention to Henry. The eye contact was uncomfortable and whilst Henry was forced to look away, Jock continued his gaze.

"Your colleagues followed me Mister Dempsey. They were harassing me, and I was forced to get onto a bus and I happened to end up outside a school in Fitzroy where they arrested me."

Henry shook his head. Jock held up his hand as a signal to his colleague. Don't say a word.

"You do know you're not allowed near schools Silas?" Jock replied.

"I had no idea that's where I was," Silas replied, still smirking. "As I said, your colleagues were watching me. Following me, on foot and in cars. I was intimidated and had nowhere to go."

Henry and Jock glanced at each other. The worried look on Henry's face was evident.

"I killed them Mister Dempsey," Silas stated boldly. He leaned forward again on his chair, his elbows on the desk, "I killed every last one of them."

Jock could feel his heart racing.

"Who did you kill Silas?"

"The ants. They were all over my house. In my backyard, covering the pathways. They were getting into my kitchen."

Silas laughed. Leaning back in his chair, his head tilted backward. He was enjoying and savouring every moment of his own attempts at humour. Playing them.

"Ahhh the looks on your faces," Silas continued.

Henry lowered his head, frowning. Jock got up from his chair, walking back toward the door before turning on his heels and returning to his chair, using it to prop himself up.

"You know Mister Dempsey, if you had any real evidence you would have bought me here by now."

"Have you ever met Sarah Stewart or Phoebe Davis?" Henry asked.

Silas kept his gaze on Jock, refusing to look at Henry. "I know my rights. You read them out to me earlier remember?"

"Where were you going this morning Silas?" asked Jock, continuing to press.

"Just a walk. I like looking at all the pretty ladies. Particularly in the morning, there's more of them around you know. All the school mum's taking their kids to school and going to work."

"Where were you going?" Jock repeated.

"All around Melbourne."

"Tell me specifically."

"Read me my caution and rights again please Detective. I've forgotten them already."

Jock could feel his heart rate rising. All he wanted to do was to lift the chair and ram it into Silas Crowley's face. To end the mind games and to wipe that smirk off his face.

"Tell me about your house Silas. Any hidden rooms within your home?"

Jock was looking for a change of behaviour. Trying to get a rise out of his offender. Yet Silas didn't seem to flinch. Not even a blink.

"You are welcome to come in one day and have a look. I can make you a cup of tea. Perhaps you can bring the family around for dinner."

Henry could see his detective sergeant tense up. He'd been around long enough to know when Jock's buttons were pushed and what the point of no return would be. Henry knew that line had been crossed.

"I'm going to suspend the interview," he interjected, "whilst Detective Sergeant Dempsey and I have a quick word."

Henry reached across and hit the pause button on the machine, before ushering Jock out of the interview room.

"What the fuck do you think you're doing?" Jock said, giving Henry a shove to the chest. "Don't you ever hijack my fucking interview again. How dare you ask him those questions about Sarah Stewart and Phoebe Davis. We have no evidence on Silas and if we quiz him on them now, we can't do it again later. You are a fucking amateur."

Katrina watched on, eyes wide and mouth open. Jock marched away down the hall, then stopped and turned to face them. The look of anger was still evident on his face.

"Get Crowley out of here. The interview is over."

CHAPTER 20

The Past

"ARE YOU SERIOUS!"

Olivia slammed her car keys down on the kitchen counter. "How long for?"

"I don't know," Jock responded, quietly spoken. "Maybe a month, maybe two?"

"Two months!"

"I said I don't know."

"John, I told you from the beginning that this job, this operation, was going to get us all in trouble. How do you suppose I take that much time away from work?"

Jock gave his wife a half-shrug of his shoulders. What could he say?

"Have you told Lucy?" Olivia asked, sliding open the door to the dishwasher and pulling out the dry plates.

"I've only found out today. Pauline's orders. The Serbs are going to be looking for me. For us. Particularly now that one of their own is dead. We need to get out of town for a bit. I figured a holiday would be good."

"What do you mean one of their own is dead?"

"George. Remember him? The one I was telling you about?"

Olivia muttered something under her breath, before lifting her head from the dishwasher, "A holiday would be great John, but this isn't a holiday. We are running and hiding."

"Wouldn't you rather be safe?"

Olivia turned around, slamming the tea towel down on the bench.

"I would rather not be in this position at all."

Jock stood his ground, pinning his wife with a look just daring her to continue the argument.

"What do you want me to do Olivia? This is my job!"

"That's what you always say John. You use it like it's a throwaway line. Two years ago, we had to move house. Then the girls and I had to change our last names. When does it end? Now we have to run. With no idea when we're coming back!"

"Don't say that."

"Don't say what?" She replied.

"You said girls. Plural. Don't do that."

"You know what I meant."

"You're blaming me again."

Olivia's tone had calmed. "It's not what I meant John. I meant Lucy. I'm sorry."

Jock ran his finger along the kitchen bench top, before silently easing away from the kitchen.

"John, don't walk away."

"You know what Olivia? Fuck you."

Olivia took a step back. Her hand over her mouth.

"You heard me." Jock continued. "What happened to Isabelle was out of our control. I told you that. I explained that to you. All these years later you still blame me for it."

"I didn't say that John, I swear to God I didn't say that. It was an accident." Olivia lent back against the sink. Tears welled in her eyes. She ran her hand through her hair, "we've lost it."

"Lost what?" Jock snapped.

"Trust John. Trust for one another."

Jock scoffed, pointing his index finger at his wife, "it's not lost Olivia. It was never there. You've never trusted me."

"What do you want me to say John? You continually put work before your family. You always have. Every decision you make, it's like we're not even considered."

"You told me when I started this that you would do your best to understand it," Jock replied.

"You haven't given me a chance to understand it," Olivia snapped back. "You've just dictated to us what we must do to keep our family safe. Uprooting us all the time. I've had to change jobs. Lucy has had to change schools. When does it end?"

Jock took a step toward the door, before turning back. "I think it's time."

Olivia wiped her eyes with the tea towel, "time for what?"

"I'll go," Jock began, "you stay, I'll go. But when I get back, I'd prefer it if you weren't here."

The Present

The Panda and the Bear coffee shop is Jock's favourite. It sits buried away in a small alleyway behind the hustle and bustle of Lygon Street.

He loves it for two reasons. Not many people know it's there and his colleagues can't find him.

Except on this occasion. As he glances up from his cappuccino, he watches Pauline pull up a seat. The detective inspector isn't an ordinary colleague. She knows his habits and knows them well.

"I knew I'd find you here," states Pauline, smiling. If she wasn't the same age as Jock, she'd almost pass for his caring older sister.

"What the hell happened this morning?"

Jock placed his mug neatly back down on the table.

Pauline continued. "Henry says you shoved him. I think you've rattled them this time Jock."

"I lost my cool," he replied in a low tone. "I shouldn't have done that."

"You're letting Silas get in your head. Again."

Jock rubbed at his face with both hands. Eventually resurfacing for some air. "I know he's involved. I just can't prove it."

"Forensics' asked me to authorise a DNA sample you sent them from Crowley's home. What was that about?"

"I found some hair at his house."

"At his house?"

"In his house."

"For fuck's sake Jock. That's why we have search warrants. How are you going to justify that now?"

Jock took another sip of his coffee. "I'll work something out. I always do."

"Your crew, they aren't going to keep accepting your ways of doing things. You know the superintendent wants you out. He's gunning for you, and I'm the only thing standing in your way. It's only going to be a matter of time before Marcus or Katrina make a complaint and I won't be able to simply brush it off."

"I never asked you to protect me," Jock replied confidently, "I can fight my own battles."

Before Pauline could reply, they were interrupted by the passing waitress.

"Can I get you a coffee or some breakfast?"

The waitress was young. Maybe only eighteen. Her face still riddled with acne as she spun a pen around in her hand.

"Just a latte please. One sugar." Pauline said, turning her attention back to Jock.

"You are very good at what you do Jock, no one is disputing that. It's how you do it. The organisation has changed, you can't treat your crew the way you used too. You may think they are useless, but they are only as good as the person teaching them."

Jock scoffed. "You can't train a monkey to be a brain surgeon. They're all lost causes."

"I get that you and some of them don't agree on some things, but you seemed to be developing a good rapport with the Chapman kid. What happened there?"

"He's too nosey. He struggles to follow simple instructions."

Pauline shook her head. This was quickly becoming a losing battle.

Jock put his mug down and lent in, so he was closer to his boss. "Silas knew we were following him. He knew Henry was police, he even knew Katrina's name."

"That information isn't hard to find out. Particularly if he's as smart as you say he is. Police details are public knowledge. You know that."

"He knew very quickly."

"What are you trying to say Jock?"

"I have a bad feeling about all this. Like I did ten years

ago when Nikola was deported, and half his crew got away with murder."

"You think Silas has help?"

Jock peered over both his shoulders. "Ten years ago, we caught Silas on a fluke. Circumstantial evidence and the overwhelming suggestion he was involved in the kidnappings and sex trafficking. But the big fish was Nikola. I think Nikola was paying Silas to do the dirty work, then Nikola and his crew were on selling girls and women to the highest bidder. I never found the link, but I know Nikola had police on his payroll and politicians as well."

"You saying Nikola's involved? Isn't he in Serbia?"

"He was released years ago. I don't even know if there is a customs alert on his re-entry in Australia. I wouldn't be surprised if there wasn't. The whole thing stinks of the Serbian mafia again."

Both of them sat in silence for a moment before Pauline eventually spoke.

"What do you want to do?"

Jock ran his index finger along his chin, staring at the ceiling.

"I need some time to think. If Nikola is here, I need to track him down."

"That's the dumbest thing you've said so far," Pauline replied. "He knows who you are now. If he sees you, he'll kill you."

"That's a risk I'm prepared to take."

"No Jock. Let me look after it. I'll make some calls," she added.

Jock shook his head and let out a sarcastic chuckle. "How could you be so naïve? If he's back in Melbourne, it means he'll have contacts. He'll have all his people working in the various pockets that he had before. This means his fingers will be in every pie, in every organisation."

"You need to let this go Jock, it's not healthy. He was arrested, as was his crew. Danny did a good job, he cleaned them up and sent most of them to trial. Those ties and networks are gone," Pauline responded, accepting her coffee from the waitress and lowering it down onto the table with two hands.

"You still think Chapman did a good job?" he laughed.

"You don't?"

"He picked and chose who he wanted arrested. Who he charged. Nikola did less than a year in a minimum-security prison then got deported upon the request of the Serbian government. His two right-hand men made deals and got away with community corrections orders. Tell me that justice was served Pauline?"

"You know that's how it goes Jock. We don't always get the desired outcome. That part is out of our hands."

"You don't find that a coincidence?"

"Your paranoia is on a whole new level Jock. We all work together. As a team. No one is out to make anyone else look bad or let crooks off the hook. We get them to court and let the judicial system do the rest. That's our job." Pauline replied, taking a sip of her coffee.

Jock put both his palms down on the table and lifted himself up off his chair.

"How many times do we need to go over this Pauline? I've told you how I felt about it ten years ago. My feelings haven't changed. It's not a coincidence that our undercover operation was shut down right when we were beginning to expose this paedophile or sex trafficking ring or whatever the fuck you want to call it. It's not a coincidence that Chapman took the reins and arrested all the wrong people, while the main players in this whole thing walked away. It's no coincidence that Crowley is back to his old ways and is one step ahead of us and it's not a coincidence that Nikola hasn't been seen or heard from again and no one seems to care."

Jock stopped for a moment and peered around the café. Thankfully it was relatively empty, except for an elderly couple sitting in the opposite corner enjoying a slice of cake together. Now however, they were looking up at him to see what all the commotion was about.

Jock lowered his voice. "It's just the same shit again. Here I am, explaining to you what I think is happening, and here you are telling me I'm paranoid. I can see in ten years nothing has changed. I needed your help back then Pauline and you let me down. I lost my marriage; I lost my daughter. I don't know why I bothered thinking you'd help me now."

And with that, Jock let go of the table and walked out of his favourite café.

Pauline sat for a moment, staring at the wall.

As the waitress approached, she touched her arm. "Can I get this in a takeaway cup?"

CHAPTER 21

JOCK TURNED THE KETTLE ON AND RUBBED HIS EYES. Glancing up at the analogue clock hanging on the wall, the roman numerals made it clear to him it was late. Nearly midnight. He still needed his ritual cup of tea however to help ease him off to sleep.

"You just getting in now?" came a voice from the doorway.

He spun around, catching Lucy in her pyjamas standing by the kitchen door. Her hair was a mess and she appeared half asleep.

"Sorry for waking you. I tried to be quiet," he apologised.

She smiled. Something about her smile warmed him. It washed away all the hatred in the world, all the crime and evil. It made him feel more human and at ease.

"You may as well make me one too." She wandered in the kitchen and propped herself up on the bench.

"What time did you go to bed?" he quizzed, throwing her a chocolate biscuit from the open jar on the bench.

She took a bite. "About 9ish," she replied, trying to avoid dropping biscuit crumbs all over the floor, "I had a late night last night finishing off a uni assignment, so I couldn't keep my eyes open."

Jock reached up and hoisted two mugs from the overhead cupboard, gently lowering them down on the counter before filling both with a tea bag.

"When you are going back to your mum's?" he asked, quizzingly. It was in the back of his mind that Penny will likely want to come back to his house after their scheduled dinner later in the week and he didn't want another awkward encounter like the last time.

"You trying to get rid of me?" Lucy smirked, "or you hiding something? You have more women coming?"

Jock let out a nervous chuckle. She wasn't wrong.

"I'm seeing this supermodel," he responded jokingly, "I don't think you're ready to meet her yet. She's prettier than your mother and I feel you may judge me."

Lucy laughed, throwing the tea towel at him. "You're such a jerk."

He poured out two cups of tea and eased in the milk before propping himself down on the bar stool alongside his daughter. He cherished these moments. Between his work and her social life and living between parents, he was rarely able to seize such opportunities.

"What are you working on at the moment?" Lucy asked, grasping the mug with both hands.

Jock glanced down at his drink. "Nothing that exciting."

"Yeah right," she scoffed. "You're in the homicide squad and you're not working on anything exciting?"

Jock changed the subject. "I just want to apologise for not being around much."

Lucy gently smiled back at him. "You don't need to apologise dad. I know it's your job. I'll be back down again mid semester. It's fine."

Jock lowered his head, avoiding any awkward eye contact.

"I don't just mean this time. I mean all the times. I've always put work first and it's why your mother and I aren't together. I pushed her away because I felt like she didn't understand, but I've realised it's been my fault. I wasn't prepared to make work the second priority in my life."

Lucy ran her hand up and down his back. "Seriously Dad, it's okay. I love that you're passionate about what you do and I wouldn't want you to change that."

Jock looked up at her, a forced smile on his face. "It's funny. Your mother and I have very little compassion between us, yet here you are. You have more empathy, compassion and understanding then the two of us put together. You can't be my daughter."

Lucy chuckled. "After seeing what you've been up to over the past couple of weeks, I don't doubt that for a second. I'm wondering whether my mother is my real mother."

Jock gave her a light shove in the shoulder, "Cut me some slack will you? Call it a mid-life crisis."

"Well, if that's as bad as it gets, I don't mind."

They both had a sip of their hot drinks, sharing each other's company without judgement or dissent.

Jock eventually spoke, leaning down against the bench. "What happens after uni? Have you thought about it?"

She nodded. "Job hunting."

"Here or Brisbane?"

"Not sure yet. Depends on who has the better house at the time. You or mum."

Jock smirked.

"I'm going to bed," he said, yawning. "I'll be out before you get up in the morning. Don't forget to turn the alarm on when you leave."

"Sure thing," she replied, easing herself off the stool.

Jock shuffled out of the kitchen and into the hallway, gradually passing the front door still juggling his mug of hot tea and the shoes he'd taken off. As he moved alongside the semi-closed shutters surrounding the door frame, he noticed the front sensor light was on.

Jock reached for the shutter, tilting it upward and that's when he saw it.

On the footpath outside his home was a silhouette.

A man. Wearing all black. A hoodie covering his face.

Staring straight at him. There was no mistaking that long black hair and facial growth.

Silas Crowley.

"What is it?" Lucy asked, passing him in the hallway.

Jock immediately closed the shutter. "Just thought I saw someone outside," he replied, not wanting to startle his daughter.

She gave him a funny look before leaning in and giving him a peck on the cheek.

"Night dad," she said, before bounding down the hallway until she was out of sight.

Jock stood for a moment, then tilted the shutters upright again. Glaring outside.

Gone.

He opened the door and wandered out into the driveway, shuffling to the footpath and glancing up and down street. Silence. Not a soul to be seen or heard.

'Strange' he thought to himself. Had he imaged it? He was beginning to doubt his own mental state. No. He had definitely seen the man standing outside his home. He was certain of this.

Jock made his way back inside, locking the door behind him. He made his way down the hall and into his room. Once again he pulled back the drawn blinds. There was no one there.

'*Two can play at that game,*' Jock thought to himself as he turned off his bedroom light

CHAPTER 22

Jock lent back in his chair. 6.23am. It was early, even by his standards. But there was work to be done and no one shared the same sense of urgency that he did.

There were copious amounts of camera footage to scour, taken from various properties in the nearby streets to Crowley's home. Anything to catch movements of the convicted criminal coming and going. If he was lucky, he'd catch a sighting of the mysterious white van.

As the clock neared 7am, Jock had felt as though he'd been in the office for nearly two hours. His eyes were burning from staring at the screen. So far there had been nothing.

"Morning," he heard a familiar voice call out. It was Blair. Jock turned his head, watching on as Blair lowered his backpack onto the ground and fired up his computer.

"Hello." Jock replied, without making eye contact.

It wouldn't be long before the rest of his crew rolled into the office, one at a time. Making themselves a hot drink of some description to start the day.

Jock got up from his desk and wandered over to Henry, resting his hand on his shoulder.

"Got a minute?"

Henry nodded without word. Getting up and following Jock out into the hallway while the others all watched on, uncertain of what was taking place.

Henry followed his detective sergeant outside into the car park. Jock stopped, leaning against an unmarked police car. He placed his hands into his pockets to shield them from the cool winter air.

"Firstly, I want to apologise for how I behaved after we bought Crowley in."

Henry's facial expression indicated he was listening intently.

"I had no right to shove you. You did what you thought was best and I shouldn't have reacted the way I did."

The apology came as a shock to Henry. In his three years in Dempsey's team, he'd never heard the man apologise, even when he was blatantly wrong. He had to fill the silence through the shock.

"It's fine," he eventually got out, "I'm part to blame. I fucked up and I'll wear that. But yes, you're right. The push was a bit uncalled for."

Jock nodded in agreeance. His lengthy discussion with Pauline and then with Lucy the night before had made him realise he had to finally acknowledge his short falls. Particularly when those around him were looking to him for guidance and leadership.

Jock gave his hand in peace and Henry took it. The two men shook on it before Jock planted his hand on Henry's shoulder. "Let's go back inside, we have work to do."

The Past

Mile Petrovic drove a red BMW. It had mag rims, dark tinted windows and a sticker on the back that read, *"warning; vehicle frequently sideways"*

It stood out and was an easy car to find. Rookie error. Particularly when you were the cousin of a well-known Serbian crime boss.

George's dying words would soon be tested. Was Mile was directly involved in Nikola's crimes? If so, to what extent?

Jock and Zoran had tracked Mile down to a small cottage on the outskirts of Melbourne. A near two-hundred year old sandstone building, rebuilt to include a large extension and a pool outside. Easily affordable when you were laundering money.

"This is it," Jock muttered, pulling up the hire car four doors down from the house. They were large properties, maybe two or three acres each. Mile's home was easy to spot, it was the only house riddled with external cameras and multiple sensor lights, all attached to an internal alarm system.

Zoran scoffed. "Stands out like dogs balls eh?"

"Anyone else likely to be home? That we know of?"

"He lives alone." Jock responded. "His ex-wife left him and went back to Bosnia about five years ago. No kids. As far as I know, he's a bit of a player, on the nightclub scene. Maybe a one-night stand here or there but nothing else that I know of. My intel's a bit scratchy."

Jock got out of the car and wandered around to the boot which he'd opened, rummaging through a backpack and retrieving two balaclava's and a small nine-millimetre revolver.

Zoran swallowed. "Here we go again."

Jock gave him a discerning look, before throwing him a balaclava. "Put that on. Just in case."

Once both men had prepared themselves, they moved at speed through the night sky to Mile's home. Jock peered over his shoulder one last time to make sure there was no one else in the street, before planting his right boot straight through the flimsy antique door, sending it flying open, with timber shards from the door trim landing on the floor.

A figure emerged from the bedroom wearing nothing but trunks.

"What the fuck?" he muttered, just as Jock had pounced, knocking the man to the ground. He pulled the revolver from his pants and pushed the muzzle against the man's temple.

"Hello Mile," Jock greeted. Smirking.

The man frowned, gritting his teeth. Much like George, his pride was taking a back seat and he wasn't impressed.

Mile responded through gritted teeth. "Who the hell are you?"

Zoran stood over Mile's head. Watching on. "We have some questions for you," he said, grinning, "and unless you want to join your friend George, you're going to answer them for us."

The Present

Jock peered down at his diary while Blair took a sip of his coffee from the disposable cup.

"Where next?"

Jock ignored him. He'd collected camera footage from

the school where his team had picked up Crowley, just to be sure the events had played out how Crowley had suggested. If a complaint was going to be made, Jock wanted to be on the front foot.

In his diary, he'd made a possible list of other places to check and scour for camera footage. One of the obvious benefits of inner Melbourne were the copious number of houses and businesses that had surveillance cameras, making it relatively easy to track the movements of individuals and vehicles. The downside was that Jock had no other avenues to make enquiries. Crowley didn't own a phone, nor did he own a car. Which made it even more challenging.

The sound of Jock's phone ringing through the car speakers startled him and from the looks of things, his partner too, as Blair nearly lost his coffee cup.

"Fuck that's loud!" he muttered, patting himself down.

"Tammy?" Jock answered, recognising the number.

"Yes John," she responded, her voice booming through the speakers. Blair reached over to turn the volume dial down a touch. "We're not all deaf," he mumbled sarcastically.

Tammy continued, "general duties at Prahran have a report for another missing girl. Fifteen-year-old, Prue Devlin. She didn't return home from netball training last night. The parents have checked in with all her friends and nearby family. No one has seen or heard from her since late yesterday afternoon. Mobile phone is switched off."

Jock gripped the steering wheel with both hands. His emotions were torn between shock and anger, particularly given his recent encounter with Silas which he thought may have been a deterrent. It now appeared to have quite the opposite effect.

"Wow," Blair exclaimed, "another one."

"Yes Einstein, another one," Jock added. "Thanks Tammy.

Can you text me the parents address and contact details; I'll go and see them while I'm on the road."

Jock pulled the car up along Lygon Street. No where near where they'd been directed to go by Tammy.

"What are we doing?" Blair glanced around, as Jock parallel parked the BMW neatly between two smaller cars.

"I have to run a quick errand on the way, wait in the car."

Jock could hear Blair let out a 'huff' as he closed the door behind him. "I won't be long," he called out to Blair, hoping he wouldn't follow.

It was a familiar part of Lygon Street. An area they'd been to just a couple of weeks ago, as Jock approached Bruno's Wine Bar, peering in the window. The sign was set to 'closed' but Jock knew that Bruno would be floating around, setting tables, folding napkins, and getting ready for trade later that afternoon.

Bruno popped up from nowhere, unlatching the door and greeting his unexpected visitor with a big smile.

"John!" he said, putting both palms out in a welcoming manner. "What brings you here?"

"Do you mind if I come inside?" Jock asked.

"Why certainly," Bruno exclaimed, ushering Jock into the foyer before closing the door and latching it behind him.

The two men wandered down the long narrow restaurant area and into an awaiting office, small enough to house just the two of them and a desk with a computer.

The monitor was switched on and the display beamed in live camera footage from the street outside.

"I already gave you all the information I had," Bruno said,

placing his hands together, "what brings you back here? Did you catch someone?"

"Not yet Bruno, unfortunately" Jock answered. "I came to see how your son was doing."

"You could have done that with a phone call my old friend," Bruno laughed. "He is doing well, given the circumstances."

"How is his cancer treatment coming along?"

"He starts more radiotherapy next month. The brain tumour didn't respond to the last round of treatment, but it hasn't grown either, so we are quietly praying and being hopeful."

Jock nodded.

"What about the costs? Of the treatment? How is that going?"

"It's not cheap John. Business is always slower in winter for us, so this came at a bad time, but we'll manage. We always find a way."

Jock reached into his coat pocket, fiddling around for the cash that he had taken from Silas' home.

"I want to help," Jock began, retrieving the money from his pocket and counting out the notes. "Will three-thousand dollars be enough?"

Bruno put his hands on his head, exhaling loudly. "I can't take this from you John. I wouldn't be able to pay you back for a long time."

Jock smiled. "Please, my old friend. You don't have to pay me back. This is a gift, a token of appreciation for everything you've done for me, for us, over the years."

"I don't know what to say?" Bruno began, his eyes welling.

Jock gave him a pat on the back. "Nothing to say Bruno. You look after your son. We'll catch up again soon and have a nice bottle of red yeah?"

"You just tell me when and I'll find my best bottle." Bruno responded, sucking back his emotion.

Jock shook his friend's hand and left him standing in the office, letting himself out and returning to the car.

"Get your errands done?" Blair asked, still watching the highlights reel from the weekend of football on his phone.

"You could say that." Jock responded, still smiling.

The Past

Mile sat on his couch. His hands cable tied behind his back. His legs tied at the ankles. A prisoner in his own living room.

"Who are you guys?" he asked nervously, "Are you bikies?"

Jock and Zoran looked at each other. Jock had to admit, Zoran looked funny in a balaclava, where only his eyes and lips were exposed.

"You have beautiful eyes," Jock stated, glaring at Zoran, "has anyone told you that?"

Zoran's eye roll was more evident now that the rest of his face was covered.

"We're police," Zoran explained, "believe it or not."

Mile laughed. "Are you fucking serious?"

Jock disappeared into the kitchen for a short moment, returning with a pair of meat scissors.

"Again? Really?" Zoran quizzed, throwing his hands in the air.

"You got a better idea?" Jock challenged.

Zoran shook it off, waving his hand at Jock and ushering him to continue.

"What are you going to do with those?" Mile asked, a waiver in his voice.

"If you can recall-"Jock began, "George's crispy remains were found, minus a thumb."

"It was you guys?"

"Sure was. How do you think we found you?"

Mile squirmed in his seat.

"What do you want? Cash? It's in a black box under my bed."

"I don't care about your cash," Jock continued, "I want you to tell us more about this sex trafficking ring."

"You're not police," Mile interrupted, "you're not allowed to do this kind of shit. Did Nikola send you? To test me? I won't say a fucking word."

"Fuck the scissors," Jock muttered, throwing them to the floor and watching them bounce on the laminate floorboards. He disappeared into the garage for a short time, leaving Zoran to awkwardly wait with their bound prisoner until he returned. Carrying a hammer.

"This is better, mixing it up a bit."

He watched again as Mile squirmed on the couch. "If I tell you anything, Nikola will kill me."

Zoran chuckled awkwardly, "Funny, that's what George said."

"If you don't talk, I'll kill you," Jock added. The three men stood in silence for a moment before Jock continued, "I won't ask again."

Mile sat, staring at Jock, then turning to Zoran. He was prepared to challenge his captors.

Jock approached, raising the hammer and swinging it directly at Mile, the metal tip connecting with his knee cap. The sound on impact was like an egg being cracked. Zoran grimaced, Mile screamed, thrashing his bound legs about from the pain.

"That was one kneecap," Jock said, standing back. "I'll make it two if you don't start talking."

"Okay okay," Mile whimpered, now lying on his back. "Show me your ID's first, so I know you don't work for my cousin."

Zoran reached into his pocket, retrieving his police identification, opening it up for Mile to see.

Mile was seemingly satisfied, nodding his head. His lips still pursed from the pain. The blood drained from his face.

"It's new," he began, "a new venture. We had some interested buyers approach us, some we knew were clearly pedo's, some were just wealthy men. They wanted girls. Women."

"Who?" Jock asked, tapping the hammer against the palm of his hand.

"Word has spread. They come from all over the world. Saudia Arabia. Spain. The Philippines. They give demands, they offer top dollar. Millions. We find the girls and we provide them, normally via Nikola's private jet. We fly them to Queensland, then they get transported by boat."

"How long has this been going?"

"A couple of months."

"Bullshit."

"Maybe a bit longer. I don't know."

"Who kidnaps the girls?"

"Some dude," Mile continued, "he's a fucking lunatic. A loner. Lives by himself. We got wind of this bloke through Nikola's contacts. We pay him in cash, normally it's about one percent, but honestly, this guy would do it for free he's that fucking weird."

"Who is he?"

"I can't tell you that, it'll fuck the entire operation. Then Nikola will know I've been blabbing. I'm the only one who knows."

Jock took two steps forward and swung the hammer again. This time, connecting with the other knee.

Mile rolled off the couch, now on the floor face down. Zoran turned to look away, it was more than he could stomach. That noise. The sound of the kneecap breaking against the metal end of the hammer.

"Fuck!" Mile cried out, rolling from his back onto his stomach. Kicking his feet into the floor, "you motherfucker!"

"Next one is to your head," Jock explained. "Who is he?"

"I don't know his name."

"I call bullshit."

"You call it what you want. We don't do names. I meet him in the park once a week to pay him. Otherwise, he delivers the girls to my crew. We supply the car. It's normally all done within a few hours."

"How do you make contact then? How do you know when he has the girls?"

"He tells me when I meet him. The guy is a pro. He'll tell us when and where the drop is made. My men go along and without fail, he is always there. Girl in toe. Each and every time."

"What sort of money is being exchanged?"

"A lot."

"Some of these girls are young kids. Do you realise this? Eleven, twelve years old." Zoran interrupted, "I should fucking shoot you right now where you lie. You're just as a big a paedophile as these men that are buying them."

"I have nothing to do with it," Mile replied, still lying face down on the floor, his head tilted to the side. His cheek pressed against the floorboards. "I pay the man and that's it. I make sure the girls are delivered. I don't even see them."

"That makes you feel better does it?" Zoran asked, a sense of rage building up inside of him.

"Just because you don't see them means it's all okay?"

"That's not what I said," Mile responded. "It's Nikola's operation. The whole thing was his idea. I just do what I'm told. We all just do what we're told. That's how this works. He'd kill his own mother if she fucked him over. You don't understand. We are paid well for what we do, but we are paid even more for our silence."

Zoran snatched the hammer from Jock's hands, running over to Mile, he raised it over his head and before Jock could process what was about to happen, Zoran swung the hammer, right into the back of Mile's skull.

Stumbling back, Zoran dropped the hammer to the floor. Mile lay motionless. Silent. His eyes were still open but the two men now noticed a pool of blood trickling beneath him.

There was a short moment of silence, before Jock eventually spoke.

"You have anger issues." He muttered, wide eyed.

Zoran was taking deep breaths. In. Out. In. Out.

"Fuck," he responded, rubbing his face with both hands. "What have I done?"

"Yep," Jock continued, "well, I did want to know more, but I guess he's not really going to answer any more questions."

"Sorry John," Zoran said, crouching down and resting his balance on his fingertips, "I don't know what came over me."

"It's been a big couple of weeks. He's no loss to society, don't worry about that."

"Fuck," Zoran muttered again. He could feel the nausea

rising in the pit of his stomach. He was going to be sick. He felt his stomach bubbling away like a volcano about to implode.

Jock glanced over Zoran, watching the colour drain from his face.

"Go and wait in the car, I'll sort this out."

Jock watched on as Zoran wandered to the front door, his head on his hands as he disappeared out of sight. Zoran was no killer, but now it was clear that this saga was affecting him just as much as it was Jock. Zoran had been suffering in silence. He rarely lashed out. Zoran was traditionally the conservative type, quiet and resilient.

Jock retrieved the hammer and proceeded to take it into the laundry, where he'd clean it with bleach before neatly placing it back in the garage where he'd found it.

He wandered throughout the house, room by room. He rummaged through the dead man's personal belongings, trying to obtain information to corroborate Mile's story. Was it true that he didn't know the kidnappers name? Or was he trying to protect the operation by only providing half the story?

The house was clean. Not a shred of evidence to suggest that the half-dressed dead man in the living room was part of a global sex trafficking ring.

Jock eventually returned to the car, removing his balaclava and gloves.

Opening up the driver's side door and getting in, he peered across at Zoran who was staring into space.

"You okay?"

Zoran nodded. "I think so. I don't know what came over me."

Jock tapped his hand on Zoran's thigh. "I'm hearing you."

"Did you clean up?" Zoran asked, snapping out of his trance.

"Not really. I figure his own people will find him first and they won't report his death to the police. We're safe on that front."

Zoran cracked a smile. "What now? All our leads are dead."

Jock started the car and held onto the steering wheel with both hands. "Nothing we can do now. Let Chapman finish what we started and hope like hell he does the right thing."

CHAPTER 23

Jenny Devlin was a mother in distress. Her daughter, Prue, was missing. So, when she opened the door and greeted Jock and Blair, bursting into tears, it was to be expected.

Nobody wanted two detectives knocking on their door, whether you were the criminal or the victim.

"Mrs Devlin?" Jock asked.

The woman nodded, wiping her eyes then her nose with a tissue.

"Do you mind if we come in? We just need to talk to you about Prue."

Jenny opened the security door and ushered both the men inside without word. Sitting on the couch was a young boy, he looked around six or seven years old and was fully engrossed in a cartoon on his tablet.

"Who have we here?" Jock asked, kneeling down beside the child.

"This is Thomas," Jenny said, wavering in her voice. "Prue's younger brother."

"Hi Thomas, my name is John but my friends call me Jock."

The little boy gave a half smile before leaning to his right, trying to see the screen beyond Jock's head.

Blair gave a snort. "The kid is a good judge of character."

Jock ignored his comments and followed Jenny into the kitchen, where he sat himself down at the dining table. Peering around the room, it was filled with photos of a happy family. Two adults and two children, which Jock could make out as Prue and Thomas. At the beach. At the snow. All dressed up for a wedding.

Jock began, unzipping his compendium. "Mrs Devlin, I know you spoke to the uniform members early today, but I wanted to run through some questions with you if that's okay?"

Jenny gave him a rapid nod of the head, still wiping away the residual tears on her face.

"Mrs Devlin—" Blair began, "when did you last hear from your daughter?"

"As I told the other police, she walks to netball practice every Thursday afternoon, it's about a kilometre to the courts. Occasionally she'll meet up with one of her team mates on the way, Belle Jacobs, but Belle has been with her family on an overseas holiday for the past couple of weeks."

"So Prue was alone?"

"Yes."

Jock took notes as Jenny spoke, eventually catching up. He glanced up at her, "over the past few days, even weeks, have you seen anything unusual? Cars parked outside your home that aren't normally there. Anything out of the ordinary?"

Jenny's eyes rolled up, deep in thought, trying to recall memories. Anything that might help.

"Not that I can think of," she replied, deflated. "But it's not like I pay attention to these things either though."

"Of course not," Jock gave her a reassuring smile.

"There is something though—" she continued. "We get along quite well with our neighbours and the young couple who live on the corner, Simon and Louise. He's in IT and he has cameras outside his home. We were chatting earlier, and he said he'd heard the news and mentioned there was a car on his footage. It appeared odd and he was going to go back and download it for you guys. Not sure if you've spoken to him yet."

Blair and Jock glanced at each other.

"Did he say what sort of car?" Jock asked.

"Yes. A white van."

Blair took his shoes off. It had been a rule in the family home since he could remember. Never wear yours shoes inside.

His parent's house was the same now as it was when he was a child. Nearly two decades ago. Although his bedroom had been turned into a guest room, and his sister's room was now a makeshift office. A place where Blair's mum could edit old family photos and transfer them from film to an electronic format. It kept her busy in retirement.

"Mum? Dad?" Blair called out.

"In the living room Blair," he heard his mum respond.

Blair wandered down to the end of the house where both his parents sat in their separate recliner chairs, the early nightly news playing in the background. His father had the newspaper open on his lap, while his mother sat with her reading glasses on the bridge of her nose, engrossed in the latest romance novel she'd likely borrowed from the library.

"What brings you here?" his mother quizzed, a smile beaming on her face.

"Just wanted to chat to dad. Shop talk," he replied.

Blair's father didn't move. Instead, he straightened out the newspaper with a flick before turning the page.

"What is it?" he eventually asked.

Blair sat down on the empty couch, retrieving his phone from his pocket which was digging into his thigh.

"I'm in John Dempsey's crew," Blair continued, "I don't think I told you last time we spoke."

His father lowered his newspaper and peered across at him. Unlike Blair's mother, Danny Chapman's glasses sat in the centre of his nose. He still looked as sharp as he did the day he retired three years ago. If anything, the time away from the job made him look younger.

"What's that idiot up to these days? Obviously still in the job?"

"He blames you for Nikola Petrovic being shipped back to Serbia."

"That's how John Dempsey operates son," Danny stated. "He blames everyone for everything, but never has the guts or the courage to take some responsibility for his own fuck ups."

"Daniel!" Blair's mother squawked.

"Mistakes. I meant to say mistakes," Danny corrected himself.

Blair smirked. His mother never liked curse words. More so now in her old age.

"What's he saying now?" Danny added.

"It's not what he says," Blair replied. "It's just the off-the-cuff remarks that he makes from time to time. I met his old partner, Zoran and between the two of them, it seems as though there's no love left in this world for you. I'm worried he treats me differently because I'm your son."

Danny folded his newspaper in half and sat it in his lap, before turning to face Blair.

"John Dempsey is dangerous," Danny went on, "he fucked up his own undercover operation by snooping around and chasing intel he couldn't corroborate. He got other members of the drug cartel killed because he got them to do his dirty work. Something he didn't want to do himself. When it came time to handover the reigns, Dempsey held back critical information and provided my team with a half-arsed statement, which meant most of Petrovic's men walked free."

Blair threw his head back into the couch cushion, peering up at the ceiling. *'Two sides to every story'* he thought to himself.

"Is he still carrying on about that?" Danny asked.

Blair sat back upright. "We've had four women, correction, girls, all abducted in the last two weeks. No leads. Same M.O as last time. He thinks it's Crowley again but can't be certain. We've got nothing because his chasing Crowley rather than focusing on the evidence and seeing where that leads us. He's trying to tie the evidence to Crowley, which has been impossible to do so far."

"Just between you and me, I think the only reason Crowley was convicted is because money changed hands," Danny offered.

"Are you saying Dempsey paid someone?"

"The evidence was all circumstantial back then. I saw the brief of evidence; Robbo asked me to glance over it before he sent it to the OPP. It was weak. All he had was Crowley being in the wrong place at the wrong time without reasons and one particular victim that Crowley had followed not long before she vanished."

"You think he had him in the gun back then too?" Blair asked.

"I know it. Sounds like history is repeating itself. The detective inspector is his mate, so she won't pull him up. You're best to get out of that crew and into another. He's bad news and he's no good for your career."

Blair rubbed his chin, peering at the television and ignoring the commercial for potato chips.

"There's something about him though dad. He's intriguing. He's very knowledgeable and in some ways.... mysterious."

"Don't be an idiot son. There's nothing mysterious about him. The man is just plain corrupt and incompetent. He'll get you in the shit with him. It's only a matter of time."

"What should I do?" Blair asked.

"Do what I did," Danny answered. "Wait for him to fuck up, then pull the rug out from under him and take all the glory."

CHAPTER 24

Jock peered down at his phone. It was the third time Lucy had called in a matter of minutes.

He ignored Blair's persistent questions in the passenger seat and answered the call. "What is it honey?"

"Dad, you need to come home," she said. Jock could sense a nervousness in her voice.

"Is everything okay?"

"There's a guy at the door who claims to be an old friend. He is creeping me out. I told him you weren't here, but then he said he'd wait out front till you got home. I don't know what to do. He's been here fifteen minutes just sitting on the step."

Jock's heart was racing. He didn't care about himself, but when trouble loomed for his daughter, his adrenaline kicked in. He could feel a sense of rage building up inside of him.

"What does he look like?" Jock quizzed.

"I dunno dad, he's an older guy. Dark, short hair and wearing a blue suit. Looks European. He's got an accent."

Blair lent forward in his chair. "Nikola."

Jock nodded agreeingly.

Nikola had found him.

ADAM NIKSIC

After all these years.
He'd returned.

Jock couldn't recall the last time he'd driven so erratically. Ducking and weaving through peak hour traffic and over taking cars using the median strip. He had turned a thirty minute drive to his home into just eight minutes.

He parked the unmarked BMW outside his home. Getting out of the car, the first thing to hit him was the smell of the brake pads burning. The second, was Nikola standing by his front door. A half smile on his face. He looked as though he was enjoying the fact that he'd found Jock's home. His chest was puffed out, his stance oozed confidence. Arriving unannounced on the doorstep of a detective didn't faze him.

"Wait in the car!" Jock demanded, peering across at Blair and slamming the door.

He opened the small white picket gate and wandered up the short garden path to his door.

"Mick Murphy?" Nikola asked, still smirking, "or John Dempsey? Which do you prefer?"

"What the fuck do you want?" Jock asked abruptly. His hand instinctively resting on his firearm.

"Just came to say hello. Are we going inside for a coffee?"

"You're not welcome anywhere near my home."

"Funny that," Nikola began, "if I can recall, you were invited into my home. Where's your manners?"

"I don't have any," Jock replied abruptly. The two men now standing toe to toe.

Jock could see through the corner of his eye Lucy fiddling

with the blinds, trying to get another look at the uninvited guest.

"You have a lovely daughter. How old would she be now? 18, 19?"

"20," Jock replied, "but you already know that."

"Sheesh," Nikola said, whistling, "time flies eh? They grow up so quickly."

"What do you want Nikola? Revenge? Retribution? Which is it?"

Nikola, still smiling, looked down at his shoes, then back up at Jock. "If I wanted revenge Detective Sergeant Dempsey, I would have had it many many years ago."

"So, what is it? You wanting to scare me? To show me you're back in Melbourne?"

Nikola gave a short chuckle. "I much prefer Belgrade to Melbourne, but unfortunately, I had some unfinished business here. As you know."

Jock stated, "you've got six seconds to get the fuck off my property. After that, a little scenario will play out. You're going to reach for my firearm, I'm going to fend you off, but not before you unclip it from its holster. In our attempts at wrestling for the gun, it'll go off and I'll get to put a round through your fucking head."

"That's a very violent story you've concocted, Mister Dempsey. But we both know you're not going to do that, because you're still chasing answers. Answers that you never got out of George or Mile. That's right. I know it was you."

Jock stood back; his tongue caught in the back of his throat. Nikola was right. He was desperate and still searching for the answers he craved. The desire for closure was greater than ever. Even after all these years, it was still front of his mind. How Nikola had ran his operation. What Benny had stumbled across and been killed for. Where all those kidnapped women had gone. Even now.

"What are you proposing?" Jock asked, calming himself from his previous outburst.

"I must admit Mister Dempsey, you certainly have the upper hand in this situation. My men could kill you right now, but too many of my friends would frown upon this. I need these people to keep my business operating. So occasionally, you must make deals with the devil you know? It comes with any business I suppose."

Jocks' eyes widened. "You're saying amongst your corrupt police friends and politicians, my life actually means something?"

"If it didn't, you'd be dead by now." Nikola replied coldly. "You were the only person who I ever truly feared would bring my operation to its knees. But I knew, through my associates, I could and would eventually hold your leash. And here we are. A decade on. Nothing has changed."

"Danny Chapman eh?" Jock scoffed. "Is that why you got away with everything you did back then? The planned extradition back to Serbia? The lighter sentence?"

"Sadly, Daniel Chapman was never on my side. His bosses, however, are a different story. Being in prison for a short time meant my operation could continue through the people I trusted. My deportation to Serbia meant I could re-group and return, knowing the storm had passed. Sometimes you must make small sacrifices for the greater good. To come back bigger and better."

"If you knew my true identity all that time, why didn't you call me out?"

Nikola ran his fingers through his slick hair. "Kudos to you Mister Dempsey. We didn't know. No one did. You and your team kept it wrapped up nice and tight. It wasn't until the end that my police sources began to unravel your little side hustle. That's when we decided it would be easier to remove you from the equation, then to stop me from continuing my business."

Jock nodded along. He knew it. He had known it all along that someone had found out and put a stop to it. Someone within police command.

"So, you're back. I'm going to ask again, what do you want?" Jock asked.

"I'm asking you for some mutual respect. You turn a blind eye, and our relationship will flourish. You can go back to investigating murders and I'll go back to supporting the local economy. Employ the unemployable and keep the streets safe. Just as I did back then."

Nikola's grin widened. He was quite proud of his proposal. It was an offer Jock couldn't refuse.

"Sadly, I'm too invested to consider your business proposal," Jock replied. "It's become personal. It became personal ten years ago and I blame you for all of it."

The two men stood in silence for a moment, pondering the stalemate before Jock continued.

"What if I don't back down? What happens if I keep coming for you?" Jock questioned.

Nikola's smirk vanished; his frown returned. He placed his hands in his pockets.

"Well, as the old saying goes Mister Dempsey, I know where you live and what's important to you. You need to decide which battles you want to fight. Sure, you may win one or two, as you did back then. But ultimately, you'll never win the war. Take your time to at least consider my proposal, as somewhat of a peace offering. Then let me know what you want to do. My business card is under your front door."

Nikola walked past Jock, brushing his arm as he made his way down the short garden path and onto the street, disappearing out of sight.

Blair got out of the car, watching Jock for a reaction. The front door opened and Lucy emerged. A deep frown evident on her face. "Who was that dad?" she asked, biting her fingernails. Her hands trembling with fear.

"No one you need to worry about darling," he replied. "He's a nobody."

The inspector paced up and down her office, her hands behind her back, while Jock sat in the chair opposite her desk.

"You need to calm down Pauline," Jock muttered.

Jock could feel his phone ringing in his suit pocket. Pulling it out and looking at the screen.

It was Jade. That was the second time today. This time she'd left a message. He decided he'd listen to it later. She was likely wanting to catch up. Now wasn't the time.

"Nikola Petrovic turns up on your doorstep and bribes you to leave him alone or he'll kill your family. What's there to be calm about?" The inspector's voice was higher pitched than usual. "What are we going to do?"

"On the record? Nothing. There's nothing we can do. He has the police minister in his back pocket and senior police right here at the crime department likely on his payroll. We can't go any higher."

Pauline stopped pacing for a short moment. Shaking her head. "You just said on the record? What about off the record?"

"I deal with this my way."

Pauline shook her head. "What does that even mean? You

want to go to prison for murder? People like Petrovic don't just fall off the face of the earth without anyone coming to look for him. It won't take long before it's traced back to you Jock."

"You let me worry about that."

"No John. I won't let you do that. It's absurd. We don't live in the wild west. I think we need to keep this by the book. We need to report it to command as a threat. Get you on a plane and out of here, with Lucy. Somewhere safe until we can establish where the ties are within the organisation. You let me look after that. I trust Johnno, I've worked with him long enough. And your crew."

John tilted his head back and let out a laugh. It caught the detective inspector off guard. He sat back upright in his chair. A stern look on his face.

"Same old Pauline. It's like we're in the café all over again having the same conversation. Again, and again. You're living in a world where things are done through policy and procedure and the world abides by the legislations that are written. Sadly, I don't live in your world. I've seen firsthand what happens when it blows up in your face. We bring criminals to justice, but only the dumb ones. The smart ones know the tricks of the trade. They know how to get around our investigative techniques and money speaks many languages. People will sell their soul for the right price. It's human nature. Instinct. You can tell professional standards command, or internal affairs, or whatever they are called these days, but they are a toothless tiger. Nikola and those that he's paid off only know one language. It's death and destruction. He'll stop at nothing to keep his business running as smoothly as possible and I'm just a goldfish in a pond to him. An insect he'll more than happily stand on to continue running things as he always has. The only thing that has saved me thus far is the uniform that I wear. They'd be too big a fall out if a police member was killed and clearly he's made deals with people in high places. But he's warning was clear as day. If I keep sniffing, correction, if WE keep sniffing around, he'll do whatever it takes to save his business."

Pauline simply stared back at Jock. Her mind trying to process everything he'd just said. Her eyes wide and her face pale. She didn't know what to say. What Jock was saying was true, but she did not want to believe it. She still believed in a world where things could be made right by honesty. Perhaps this was the exception. No matter what she said, or did, she couldn't see a way around Jock's proposal.

"What do you propose John?" she eventually asked. "Is there a way to flush out the people on his payroll? Find a way to expose them?"

Jock's smile had returned. He lent back in his chair. "Now we're on the same page. That's a great idea and I think I've got the right angle in which to do it."

He got up and walked to the door.

"You've given me an idea," he said, winking at her, "I just need to send a text message to someone I know first."

CHAPTER 25

Owen Hansen was in a bad mood. The fact that he was sitting in his car on the top floor of the Alfred Hospital car park in Melbourne at nearly midnight just added to this. He would have preferred being at home, in his bed.

He tried some deep breathing. For some reason, he felt nervous. It had been a long time since he'd felt this way. He'd ran the local state seat of Melbourne for three terms, this one being his fourth. He was one of the longest serving members of any political seat in the state, not to mention holding the position of Police Minister for the majority of that time. He'd even taken on other portfolios at times to boost his political career and popularity. The ambition was to be Premier one day. Maybe enter federal politics. He was only young still. Forty-five was young in politics. But his wide ambitions came at a cost. Two divorces and his retirement benefits stripped away and paid to his ex-wive's meant money was tight. At his age, he had to think of his future. Time wasn't on his side.

As Owen was deep in thought, the passenger door opened abruptly and a figure entered, taking a seat.

John Dempsey.

"Who are you?" Owen asked. The build-up of rage had returned. This unwanted visitor demanded to see him at this unholy hour, bribery bringing them together.

"What does Nikola want this time?" he asked, red faced.

Jock smirked. "You don't know me do you?"

Owen shook his head.

"Over a decade ago, I ran an undercover operation into Nikola's drug syndicate. The Serbian mafia. Drug trafficking. Human sex trafficking. Paedophilia. All the good stuff."

Jock watched on as the blood drained from the politician's face. He'd been expecting someone from Nikola's crew. Instead, now he wasn't so sure. It made him nervous.

"I'll take that silence as you acknowledging that you know who I am," Jock continued. "You made some calls to police command and had my operation pulled. Who told you about it?"

Owen took his eyes off Jock, peering out into the darkness of the car park. "I don't know what you're talking about. I think you have me mistaken for someone else."

Jock twisted his body to face Owen. "Let me re-jog your memory," he continued, "Nikola took me for a tour of his newly opened bar. March 2012. The private function room upstairs. Invitation only. The place was a buzz with flowing top shelf whiskey and topless women. You can imagine my dismay when he took me over to one of the private booths and here was the police minister, the famous Owen Hansen. Cocaine all over his nose and two women straddling him like a twenty-year old university student during orientation week. Must have been after your last divorce. I can't imagine your wife at the time would have approved."

"You have no proof that was me," Owen said calmly.

"Aside from another eyewitness, you're right. It's only

two against one. An undercover cop giving evidence in court against a politician. I wonder who'd win that battle?" Jock stated sarcastically.

Owen blinked his eyes in rapid succession.

"What do you want?"

"I want to know who tipped you off about our operation."

"I can't tell you that."

"Why not?"

"Because it jeopardises all of my work. Everything I've done. My entire political career."

"What work would that be?" Jock asked, with a sarcastic tone.

"You need to get out of my car," Owen demanded, "before I call the police."

Jock reached into his back pocket, retrieving his badge. "No need. They are already here."

Owen's face went red. "You've got some balls detective."

Jock reached for his holster, unclipping his firearm and pointing it at the police minister.

"I don't have time for your bullshit," Jock went on. His voice surprisingly calm. "No one is going to miss a corrupt politician. Particularly one who shoots himself in the head in his own car. The irony is we're parked on the rooftop of a hospital. Although a bullet wound to the head tends to be uncurable."

Owen exhaled loudly. Gripping the steering wheel, he could feel the tension building up inside of him. The rage had turned to exhaustion. He was tired. He knew this day would come, but he'd been in denial, presuming he had covered all bases to avoid such a confrontation. Corruption had a way of catching up with you.

"I don't remember who tipped me off," Owen began, "it was a long time ago. A lot has happened since then."

"You smell that?" Jock asked, peering around the inside of the car. "Smells like bullshit." He smirked at his own joke whilst pushing the gun up to Owen's temple. "You're going to have to make yourself remember."

"I have no idea who you are, but you have no idea what you're getting yourself into. Some things are better left buried detective," Owen continued.

"I'm all ears and I am not leaving till I get my answers. Whether that's with you dead or not doesn't faze me."

"Nikola Petrovic is a businessman. As we all are. We are all out to achieve the same goal. To make money and prosper."

"By goals you mean murder, drug trafficking and kidnapping?" Jock replied, "just so I'm on the same page."

"By goals, I mean having a lawful society. Since Nikola came to me with his proposal, our crime rate has halved. We have very little issues with motorcycle gangs and street crimes. The subtle issues he has within his own house are for him to deal with, and they don't make it to the stats sheet. His crew keep the rest of the state's organised crime in check. And the crime that comes out of his activities aren't recorded. It's a win-win for everyone. Taxpayers sleep easy at night knowing there is no crime on their streets. The drug trade continues but with only a selected few. There are less overdoses because the product is higher grade and better quality. The new business ventures Nikola has put in place means we generate revenue for the state through commercial taxes and rental income. You tell me how any of this is a bad thing detective?"

Jock shook his head; he couldn't believe what he was hearing. A politician selling his own soul for what he believed to be the greater good for society.

"What about the mum's and dad's who send their daughter off to netball training, only to never hear from her again?

Or the ten-year-old who loses her twin sister to a kidnapper, to never return home. Tell me again how these situations fit into your argument for peace and prosperity?"

"Nothing more than collateral. A small sacrifice for the greater good."

"Why do you get to play God Owen? Or perhaps it's the pay check that makes everything feel better? I think that's the real reason you've agreed to get into bed with the devil. It's not for the greater good. It's not to make you look good. Two divorce settlements has to hurt the hip pocket doesn't it?"

Owen didn't respond.

Jock pushed the butt of the gun into Owen's temple, harder than he'd anticipated. The police minister flinched, squeezing his eyes closed.

Instead, Jock released his grip, re-holstering his firearm. He grabbed at the door handle, flicking it open. He turned his body back to face Owen.

"You can tell Nikola about our little interaction."

He reached into his pocket and retrieved a business card, flicking it at Owen.

"Tell him the war has only just begun. You can give him my business card."

It had been a long day.

It was becoming harder and harder to hide his activity from the rest of his crew. Particularly Blair, who had investigated the missing persons cases by his side each day. Suddenly, the need to take up a side investigation which he kept his offsider in the dark was becoming increasingly challenging.

Jock looked at the time on his computer.

8.22pm.

He had barely had three hours sleep, replaying the interaction with Owen Hansen again and again in his head. Recalling what the police minister had told him. More importantly, he'd waged war with one of the most powerful men in the state and he'd hoped his plan would work. There was no margin for error.

He copied the last of the files he'd been working on onto the USB and safely ejected the drive.

Rubbing his eyes, he peered around the office. The afternoon crew were out on the road, and it was only him left. He felt his phone vibrating in his pocket. He was expecting a call from Penny, or even Jade. It had been a while since he'd spoken to either of them.

He peered down at the screen. It was Tammy. On her personal mobile. It must have been important.

Jock got up from his desk and stuck his head around the corner into the Analysts office. Tammy was sitting behind her computer, her mobile phone in hand.

"I'm still here," Jock muttered, holding his phone up so she could see. "What is it?"

Tammy hung up her phone, standing up from her chair.

"You're working late?" he added.

Her face was white. Jock sensed some bad news coming his way, he could read it on her face.

"It's the results of the hair you found at Crowley's house."

Jock swallowed hard. This could be it. The moment he'd been waiting for.

"And?"

Tammy continued. "The DNA taken from the hair. Well, there's no easy way to say this. The DNA markers. They belong to you."

Jock's eyes widened. "What the fuck does that even mean? It's my hair?"

"No." Tammy replied, "the results indicate that there are similarities to the DNA markers. There are signposts along the genome that link the DNA to you, but they are likely from a blood relative."

CHAPTER 26

ZORAN POPPED OPEN THE WHISKEY DECANTER AND poured two glasses. There was enough in each glass to raise the ice cubes from the surface. They now floated around in the ample liquid.

"What the fuck are you going to do?" Zoran asked Jock, returning to the living room and handing his friend a glass.

Jock had been leaning forward on the couch, his elbows resting on his knees, until he heard Zoran approach with his glass of whiskey.

He remembered Jade's message. He had to call her back. Glancing at his watch, it was nearly 11pm. Probably a bit late now. She'd be asleep. He was kicking himself. He had the time earlier and had dismissed the thought.

Taking the glass from Zoran, Jock replied. "I have a plan of attack, but I need something from you."

A wave of apprehension ran across Zoran's face. "I'm not in the job anymore John," Zoran reminded him, "I can't help you with these things like I used too. I'm past all of that. I take my skeletons to the grave, but I don't need to be creating any new ones either."

Jock shook his head. "Nothing like that," Jock replied.

"Do you still have that unregistered handgun we took to Mile's house? Back in 2012?"

Zoran hesitated for a moment. "I think I do actually. It's in my safe."

"I'm going to need it," Jock added, "with some rounds."

Zoran nodded, "I'll get it for you before you leave."

The fact Zoran didn't ask any questions or jump to conclusions made Jock relax. Zoran understood.

The two men shared a sip of their drinks. Nothing but silence radiated through Zoran's home.

Jock eventually spoke. "Do you remember when we did that warrant on that nutcase back in 2015? The army freak?"

"How could I forget?" Zoran replied, "it was like Rambo's house."

"Those grenades? You kept some of them didn't you?"

Zoran's eyes lit up. "Fuck yes! I did. They are stashed somewhere in my garage. You want them too?"

"Do you think they'll still work?"

"Time will tell eh?" Zoran laughed.

"I guess so," Jock replied, taking another sip of his whiskey.

"You know something Zoran?" Jock continued, "I never thought it would come to this."

"What do you mean?"

"I'd be left sitting here. Doing this all by myself. Alone."

Zoran's heart sank. "They don't breed them like us anymore mate. Those days are over. Now they are just corporate guinea pigs, not allowed to make decisions for themselves. They get slapped with a big textbook and told to police to it."

Jock nodded along in agreement. "I think it's better that way Zoran. Once you cross that line, you think it's okay to cross it all the time. Except one day, you cross it and you can't come back."

Zoran sat in silence. Staring into his drink.

Jock continued. "Look at me. I'm so far past that line now, that I can't see it anymore. I know we always did things with the right intentions, but I think I've come to a point now where I can't see what is right and what is wrong anymore."

"Come on mate," Zoran interjected, "you're not a drug dealer. You're not a criminal. We just bend the rules. We bend them because the criminals can and we can't. Our hand is forced. Think of how many lives we saved when Nikola was locked up. When Crowley was locked up."

Jock put his empty glass down on the coffee table, having skulled the little whiskey that was left in the tumbler.

"You know what Hansen said when I confronted him?"

Zoran shrugged his shoulders.

"He had actually convinced himself that Nikola was doing good things. For society. Running a crime syndicate means you keep crime in order. Means innocent people can feel safe. They live in their little bubble, and they believe and hear what they are told. That everything is okay. Meanwhile, behind that façade, Nikola is making money hand over fist importing cocaine and meth, controlling the dealers, controlling supply. Opening up his business to human sex trafficking. Paedophile rings overseas. But no one sees that because if you ask the politicians, it's all in order. Nothing to see here. Just move along folks."

Zoran shook his head. "Come on mate," he added, "we both know that's bullshit because we've lived it. We both know it's not that simple."

Jock got up from his seat. "Don't worry," he replied, "seeing as I've crossed that line, I may as well now make the most of it. There's no going back now eh?"

He followed his last comment with a wide grin and the two men exchanged a smile.

Jock continued, "Now you need to find me that gun."

Silas Crowley's house seemed darker at night. Darker than usual.

Jock pulled his car up at the front of the property. Turning the engine off. He sat for a moment, deep in his own thoughts.

He glanced at the digital time on the dashboard that slowly faded as the car powered down.

12.10am.

It had been a long night. An emotionally and mentally draining one.

Jock reached across onto the backseat, rummaging through his kit bag until he felt the wooden handle. The kitchen knife. He retrieved it from the bag, sliding it into the back pocket of his pants.

Jock opened his door, being sure to latch it quietly so no one could hear it close.

He could see a light on inside the home coming from the living room. Jock entered via the gate, just as last time, making his way down the side of the house and in through the rear door. Once again, it was unlocked.

As Jock turned his back, he quietly closed the rear door. Until he heard a voice over his shoulder.

"Welcome Mister Dempsey."

He knew the voice. But it still sent an eerie shiver down his spine.

"For what do I owe this pleasure?"

Jock turned around slowly. Silas was standing in the entry

to his living room. The only light being emitted from the television behind him. The rest of the house lay in darkness. It was hard to make out his figure, with his long black hair and dark clothing. He looked refreshed, like he'd recently showered.

"We need to talk," Jock replied.

Silas smiled. The yellow of his teeth broke the darkness.

"Detective, before we go any further, I wish to express my disappointment in the police force, and specifically, you and your team. I don't appreciate you and your crew entering my home when I'm not here."

Jock kept a straight face. He opted not to respond to Silas' comments.

"Entering my home without a warrant won't change anything detective."

"Oh I beg to differ," Jock replied. "You see, it helps me implicate you for all those missing girls. And for Isabelle."

Silas tilted his head. Appearing confused. His eyebrows meeting in the middle.

"Ten years ago, Silas. You took our Isabelle. It was her hair that I found in your little dungeon under the floor. You had her here didn't you?"

"I don't bring the girls here Mister Dempsey, you should know that."

Jock could feel the rage burning inside of him. All the round-about answers and mind games. He leapt toward Silas, grabbing him by the throat and pinning him against the living room wall. His thumb pressing deep into Silas's throat.

"Harming me won't change anything detective," Silas said, through gasping breath.

"Where are they!" Jock yelled; tightening his grip. The colour of Silas's face went from pink to a deep shade of red.

Despite him struggling for air, Silas couldn't wipe the smile from his face. He couldn't reply, instead, focusing on keeping the air flowing into his lungs.

Jock eventually loosened his grip, letting go and taking a step back. He took his firearm from its holster. A familiar action. Pointing it at Silas.

"What did you do with Isabelle?"

"Wherever she is, she's in a better place now." Silas said, rubbing at his throat. The smile still evident on his face.

"You took her from us," Jock began, "My daughter. You have no idea what that did to my family. To me."

"I did my time Mister Dempsey," Silas replied. "I was punished. You should move on now and focus on Sarah. On Kylie and Prue."

"Where did you take them?" Jock demanded, keeping his firearm pointed at Silas.

Silas put his index finger to his lips, pressing against them. "Sssshh" he whispered, "it's a secret."

His smile returned, and along with it and overwhelming sense of pure evil. His eyes were glazed as he stared at Jock.

Jock took a step back. Crowley was like no one else. He had no sense of remorse. He wasn't human. Where Jock could feel the emotion bubbling inside of him, Silas continued to play games and his never ending smirk indicated he was enjoying every moment. Jock had lost Isabelle when she was only ten years old. Lucy's twin sister. Taken whilst she played at the park with her sister, just a stone's throw from the family home. Never to be seen again.

Jock could recall the events in his mind like they were only yesterday. He recalled Pauline trying to take the investigation from him. It had become personal. The emotion and the attachment would mean Jock couldn't think straight. He'd want justice at all costs. In hindsight, that's exactly what he got. For not only Isabelle, but for the other victims.

He thought back to Blair picking up the photo frame in his home and the way in which he brushed off Blair's questions. Nobody else needed to know what had happened. Even ten years on, it still hurt as much as it did all those years ago. The pain never went away.

He thought back to Olivia blaming him. The work he did, bringing it home with him. He was the reason Isabelle was gone. Silas wanted to make a point, he wanted to hit Jock where it hurt most. Taking his own daughter out from under his nose. There would be no greater triumph. Isabelle was the trophy.

Jock snapped back from his trance, staring deep in Silas eye's.

"Are you going to shoot me Mister Dempsey?" Silas asked, jokingly, "You're not allowed to do that. That's not playing by the rules."

For the first time since he'd arrived at Silas' home, Jock saw clarity. The rage had diminished, and he felt a sense of calm wash over him. After ten long years, the lost marriage, the anguish of losing his daughter. Of having to explain it all to Lucy. Of watching her grow up without her sister. Jock felt at peace.

It was exactly as Silas had outlined, *playing by the rules.*

Jock must have smiled, as Silas' facial expression had changed somewhat. He now looked puzzled, reading Jock's expression.

"Thank you Silas," Jock began, speaking calmly. "You have helped me see clearer."

Silas tilted his head. His long hair lapping against his shoulder, "How so Mister Dempsey?"

"I don't play by the rules."

With that, Jock closed his eyes and pulled the trigger.

CHAPTER 27

In the inner suburb of Carlton, it was a quiet street where Silas Crowley lived. His neighbours were none the wiser that they were living alongside a convicted sex offender and paedophile.

Except tonight, the street was a buzz with red and blue lights and crime scene tape. Roadblocks preventing anyone who wasn't a resident from entering or exiting the street.

Inside the house, Jock stood by the kitchen door, watching his colleagues from major crime scene take photos. Photos of Silas's dead body, still laying as it was on his living room floor. A pool of blood directly beneath him where the bullet round from Jock's gun had pierced the skin. Jock couldn't help but admire his shot. One round. Centre mass. Dead. Silas wouldn't have suffered. Not much anyway.

Aside from the body, there was something else about Silas that was different.

There was no smile.

Jock glanced down at his watch. 1.45am.

Blair stood by the detective inspector. She was still half asleep. The only thing worse than not getting enough sleep, was having your sleep cut short.

"What the hell happened here John?" she asked, scanning the room. She'd attempted to re-dress herself in the same suit she'd worn that day, except Jock could tell it had been thrown around and was now yesterday's clothes.

"I came to see Silas," he replied. "He pulled a knife on me and I shot him. Not much more to tell."

Pauline watched on as a police member from major crime scene walked past them, a kitchen knife sitting neatly in a clear plastic evidence bag.

Blair's eyes widened when he saw it. The wooden handle. He glanced across at Jock, trying to establish some form of eye contact, except Jock looked away. Blair knew he'd seen that knife before in Jock's bag. He swallowed hard. Now was not the time.

"What the hell were you doing here at midnight?" Pauline's voice drowned out Blair's thoughts.

"I wanted to talk to him, about the hair I'd found in his basement."

"The hair you seized from your illegal entry to his home?"

"It was Isabelle's hair Pauline. DNA confirmed it."

Pauline raised her hand, putting it to her mouth.

Blair glanced at both of them, darting his eyes from one to the other. "Who is Isabelle?"

Neither of them responded.

"We need to talk outside," Pauline demanded. "Before professional standards command get here."

Jock nodded, following his superior outside into the rear yard, where they were met with a quieter surround, away from the all the activity inside.

"This doesn't look good John," she continued. "You can't come to a suspect's home, at midnight, by yourself and shoot him dead. Regardless of the circumstances. This is messed up. It's all wrong."

"They can go for me as hard they like," Jock responded. "That's the truth."

Pauline shot him a nervous look. He knew that look. She was worried.

"Pauline, you don't need to worry about me. I'll go back and make my statement. Wait for the interview. It's fine."

"You'll need to give major crime scene your firearm."

"I know," he replied, "I know the drill. This isn't my first rodeo."

She gave him a short smile. Perhaps the fact that Jock was so calm was assuring her what he was telling was the truth. Needless to say, she was still concerned.

"I need to go back inside," she replied, turning on her heels.

"Hey Pauline," Jock called out to her.

She turned, glancing at him over her shoulder, making out his silhouette in the moon light.

He smiled. That she could see.

"It's finally over."

Jock poured himself another drink. In a couple of hours, it would be morning, and Lucy would be up. Starting another day, getting ready for uni and applying her makeup. Sending him a text message abusing him for skipping breakfast with her, which he had done for three days in a row.

He put his feet up on the table, leaning back in the chair and allowing himself to take a deep breath, before taking a sip of his whiskey.

He knew the likelihood that the drink he'd had at Zoran's

would appear in his urine sample he would have to provide to the investigating detectives. There was nothing he could do now. The test would likely come back positive and raise a whole new set of questions. Perhaps he could tell them he drank it from Silas' collection while he waited for backup to arrive. The thoughts of what could happen running rampant through his head. He was still trying to process the events of the evening.

He thought about what he could do instead of being a detective. Maybe take up a trade? He was always good with his hands, but who would want to employ a fifty-something apprentice?

Pulling his phone from his pocket, he'd forgotten about Jade's phone calls. All afternoon and early evening she'd tried to reach him, leaving two messages now.

He was a shitty friend. Or friend with benefits? Whatever they wanted to label it. He still wasn't sure how he felt dating a psychologist. Particularly one who had now met his daughter.

Jock pressed the play button on the message. Jade's voice came through the phone's loudspeaker.

'Hi John, it's just me. I met with that client again that I was telling you about when I was at your place last week. I'm a bit concerned actually and that's why I wanted to talk to you. He's been diagnosed as schizophrenic, with delusional and narcissistic tendencies. Today he mentioned your name. He said he was taking great pleasure in taking you on some sort of journey, making you believe he had done something. Something horrible. I'm afraid he's been fabricating the entire story. He told me how he dreamt of kidnapping young women just to see you. He seems to be fixated on you for some reason. He referred to you by name today John which he has never done before. Then he snapped because he seems to think you've been in his house twice in the last couple of weeks. Call me back as soon as you can. I'm worried now. It's getting a bit close to

home and I have some concerns on what he might do next. I fear he's not on his medications and being a schizophrenic, he's delusions can get quite worse. Call me."

Jock stopped, lowering his drink down on the table. He played the message again.

The key words, resonating in his mind. Repeatedly. *'Fabricated'* and *'story'*.

Silas had never kidnapped those women.

If what Jade was saying was true, Crowley was nothing more than a stock-standard nut case. A man on another planet to the rest of us, believing his own stories. His own lies. Getting his kicks out of living a life that isn't his.

Jock should have listened to Jade's message when he had got it. How could he be so ignorant? He'd been caught up in his own world. His own agenda. How could he have been so ignorant?

Jock sat back in his chair, his hands on his head. A deep exhale.

Silas Crowley, was an innocent man.

He'd killed an innocent man.

CHAPTER 28

Jock rubbed at his face. Being awake all night was starting to take its toll. He was tired and his eyes were heavy. Driving through peak hour traffic didn't help. Each time he came to a stop, he felt his head getting heavier, wanting to stop. To take a break. To sleep.

The sound of his phone ringing through the car speakers woke him from his micro nap.

It was Pauline. She was either awake very early, or much like him, hadn't been to sleep yet. He was thinking it was likely the latter.

"Pauline." Jock answered.

"I've just spoken to the superintendent," she said without intro. "They're coming for you Jock. He accepts that Silas might have pulled that knife on you, but even if they can make the shooting justified, the Coronial inquest and the internal investigation is going to be tough and rocky road."

Jock sighed. His shoulders slumping. He'd dodged bullets all of his career. Thirty years. Fittingly, it would be the murder of an innocent man that would finally sink him.

"I know Pauline," he replied without argument. "I know."

There was a short silence at the other end. He assumed it was Pauline trying to understand why he wasn't arguing.

"Look John," she eventually spoke, "I can get you a secondment with the federal police. Get you out of here for a while. At least while this blows over. The coronial inquest will take some time. It's going to depend on what the Assistant Commissioner wants to do with you."

"I'll wear whatever they throw at me," Jock replied, "I needed to make things right Pauline. I just did."

Jock wasn't sure if it was because he was sleep deprived, or because the emotion of the events of the past twelve hours had just sunk in. He could feel an overwhelming sense of regret and empathy. Tears welling in his eyes, he had to say something. The silence had become awkward over the phone, but it would be the detective inspector that spoke next.

"I'll do what I can Jock. Just, look after yourself."

Jock hung up from the call. Wiping his face again, he had to focus. Now was not the time to fall into a heap. He needed to know more. He still had unfinished business. The task wasn't over. Not yet anyway.

In the eight months they'd been 'seeing' each other, Jock had never been in Jade's home. But now was not the time to feel uncomfortable or carry any of the other emotions or uncertainties that came with this strange feeling.

It was close to 7am and he'd caught her getting out of the shower, using the key to her home that she gave him, that'd he never had to use.

"Sorry," he mumbled, catching her off guard. "I needed to talk to you, about your message."

With her towel still wrapped around her body, she gently ran her hand down his face. "Sure thing," she replied. "Let me put some clothes on and I'll boil the kettle."

"How long has he been your patient?" Jock asked, opting to sit at the kitchen bench rather than the sofa, so he didn't fall asleep.

"Just over a month now, he comes in once a week."

"By choice?"

"He was referred to me by the Justice Department. I think it was part of his treatment post sentence."

"And you didn't think to tell me?"

Jade frowned, leaning against the bench, "I don't read up on all the finer details John, I rely on the patient to tell me their story. They choose to disclose what they want. That's how it usually works."

Jock shook his head. "Fuck me," he mumbled under his breath. "So what exactly did he say?"

Jade thought for a moment, trying to play back the appointment in her mind. "He said, in no uncertain terms, that he'd been playing with you. He knew you were investigating him, so he played up for it. He told me about the visit to the school and told me how you and your team had gone into his home when he wasn't there."

"There it is again," Jock muttered.

"What?"

"He said the same thing last night," Jock recalled the conversation with Silas, "me and my team had been in his home. He said that last night, but we hadn't been in his home. It was only me. The one time."

"You saw him last night?" Jade asked.

Jock placed the mug down on the kitchen bench, rubbing at his face. "I wish now I had of gotten your message before I went to his house."

"What did he say to you?"

"He talks in circles. Never gives you an answer. He plays these mind games and finds ways to antagonise you."

He was getting frustrated again at just the thought of it.

Ten years ago.

Now.

"It's part of his mental health condition John. He's not well. He is a very sick man. He makes things up in his head as he goes, that's why he can't give you an answer, because he doesn't have one. He's delusional. He plays along and gets his kicks out of getting you riled up. He wants that raw emotion to come to the surface. It gives him motivation to keep going."

"He still could have kidnapped all those women," Jock stated, "I know he did it back in 2012 and I know he was somehow involved again this time."

"I don't think so John," Jade argued. "He can't give you exact details because he didn't do it. He makes it up as he goes along. Think back to all your discussions with him. At any point in time, did he ever talk specifics? Provide finer details?"

Jock shook his head. Despite the fact he was trying to sell it to himself, he knew he was drowning in his own denial. With Jade's clarity came the facts that he'd missed. A seasoned detective who was so far down the vigilante path he'd failed to see the evidence right in front of his own eyes.

"I have to go," Jock said, jumping up from his stool, "I have some other work I have to do."

"How did it end last night? Your conversation with Silas?" Jade quizzed, following him to the door.

Jock turned and gave her a kiss on the cheek.

"You don't want to know."

Henry scrolled through his phone. It's what he did to kill time.

Leaning back against his car in the large complex car park opposite the police station. A morning text message from Jock, requesting they meet made him feel uneasy. He had known Jock for three years, and while they had a mutual trust in one another, they tended to stay out of each other's way. It was better for everyone this way.

He knew Jock did not trust Marcus, nor Katrina. They often didn't agree with his agenda and his way of doing things. Henry often played the role of peace maker. He understood why some things had to be done a certain way. Jock being physical with him only a few days ago still sat fresh in his mind. He'd made his peace with it, understanding that the heightened state of emotions was primarily what was at play. It wasn't personal. He was semi glad it was him on the receiving end of it. If it had of been Marcus, things could have ended differently.

Henry could hear a car screeching its way around the car park from below. He clicked his phone off and slid it back in his pocket, in time to see Jock's BMW pull up directly beside him. The passenger window came down and Jock's face appeared from the driver's seat. "Get in."

Henry opened the door and folded himself in half to slide into the passenger seat, before Jock continued along through the car park until they reached the roof top. An isolated location with no one around.

"Get out of the car," Jock demanded. Putting the vehicle in park and switching it off.

"Why can't we talk in here?" Henry quizzed.

"Haven't I taught you better than to talk about personal things in police cars?"

"Oh right. Listening devices." Henry replied rolling his eyes. Jock and his paranoia. As if the internal investigators had nothing better to do than bug police cars.

He followed Jock through the car park to the opposite side of the roof top, where they stopped. Jock leaning against the railing, overlooking the city from twelve stories up.

"Why are we here John?" Henry asked, taking his spot next to Jock. Elbows resting on the metal railing.

"I need a huge favour from you."

Henry chuckled, half-heartedly. "I get nervous when you ask for favours."

Jock turned back around. "I know I haven't been the best detective sergeant for the crew. We've always had our differences and I was never easy to get along with."

"Understatement of the century," Henry stated, still smiling.

Jock reached into his pocket, retrieving a USB stick and reluctantly handing it over to Henry, opening up his palm and sliding it in, before rolling his fingers over it.

"This favour will be just as big for you as it is for me. This will make your career. On this drive is everything you're going to need to charge Nikola Petrovic and everyone in his crew."

"Holy shit John!" Henry exclaimed, pursing his lips and exhaling a whistle. "How? Why?" he stuttered.

"It can't be me that does this. I'm too entrenched in this and my reputation is tarnished. I'm worried the powers above will expect this to come from me. It'll catch them off guard if you drive this. On the USB is a statement that I've scanned in detailing my involvement, conversations, and basically everything I've done relating to this investigation from start to finish. There's also digital recordings. There is enough there to make arrests anyway, but for god's sake, do this properly. Don't show anybody else."

"Why not?" Henry asked, sliding the USB into his pocket.

"Because I still haven't worked out who we can trust within police command. When you open the drive, you'll see why."

Henry nodded.

"What about Blair?"

Jock shook his head, turning back around and placing his hands deep into his pockets.

"Blair means well, and he's a good kid. But he doesn't know what he's walking into. You've been around a lot longer and you've seen this stuff before. I know I can trust you to do this and do it properly. The Chapman name just doesn't sit well with me, not after his old man made a mess of this all those years ago. The inspector knows all about this. She will help you get this over the line."

Henry rubbed his face.

"This is huge Jock."

Jock tilted back his head and looked to the sky; his grin widened. "It sure is mate. But don't fuck this up. You'll only get one shot at it. I need to add, you've only got two weeks. After that, the media will know and this will be on the front page of every newspaper in the country."

Henry stood in silence for a moment, trying to process what was about to happen. Henry had known about Jock's past, with Nikola Petrovic, his undercover operation. But it was all rumours and whispers. Nobody ever had the opportunity to sit down and discuss it with the man himself. Perhaps they were too scared of what the response may be. Perhaps they just didn't want to know.

"Why have you decided to do this? He eventually asked. "Why now?"

Jock glared out over the city, taking in the view. Closing his eyes and letting the cool city breeze brush against his face.

"You know what Henry? I decided I wasn't prepared to go to war."

CHAPTER 29

Zoran fumbled for his keys. He always managed to have them in the opposite pocket to his groceries.

'For fucks' sake' he muttered under his breath, lowering down his bags and retrieving his house keys. He unlocked the front door and dragged the bags into his kitchen, lowering them down onto the tiled floor.

Glancing down at the kitchen bench was a house key, resting on top of an envelope.

He peered around the room, immediately noticing the newly purchased bottle of unopened whiskey he'd bought home yesterday was missing from his alcohol cart.

It bought a smile to his face. Jock had been here whilst he was out. He'd be the only one that would steal his alcohol.

Zoran recognised the key. It was to his front door. He picked up the envelope and retrieved a small note from inside.

It was from Jock.

'Won't be needing this anymore mate. Rest easy. No more battles to be had.'

And on the other side-

'p.s.—returned your gun to the safe. Yes, I know the pin number.'

Zoran stood for a moment, re-reading the note. Again and again. Despite his wild ways, Zoran always knew Jock to be his loyal friend and he knew whatever the silly bugger had gone and done would have been the right decision from him.

For both of them.

Penny's phone rang.

She glanced down at the screen. It was Jock. For the third time that morning.

It must have been important; she hadn't heard from him for a few days and it was unlike him to not check in. Even when he was busy.

She stared at her computer screen. Her mind was off, wandering, making it harder for her to finish her article that was due that afternoon.

Despite that fact she'd been summoned to the Editor's office, she took the call anyway. The article would have to wait.

"Hello," she answered pleasantly. It had been a while since they'd spoken.

"Good morning beautiful," he replied, the sound of white noise from his car emanated through the phone.

"Where are you?" Penny asked.

Jock paused for a moment, reluctant to tell her where he was. It was better that way.

"Just on the road," he replied. "Hey listen. I wanted to take you up on that offer that you made at dinner a few weeks ago. About running that article. About Silas and the Serbian drug cartel."

She smiled. Flipping her pen between her fingers. "About

time," she responded. "Why the change of heart? Something happen?"

"Lucy is on her way to the airport this afternoon," Jock continued, "she's going to drop a USB off to you on her way through."

"Oh, is she leaving?"

"Going back to her mum's. I guess I was just a shitty host." he joked.

She chuckled at his poor attempt at humour. "What's on the USB?"

"You'll see for yourself." Jock added, "but I just need a massive favour."

"Anything."

"Hold off publishing anything for a couple of weeks."

"Why is that?"

"I can't say, but it's imperative. If you don't, they'll be serious consequences."

Penny frowned, lowering the pen back to the desk. "Why don't you just give it to me then?"

"I'm not in a position to," Jock continued, "Penny. I'm leaving Melbourne and I won't be coming back for a long time. I'm sorry I've had to tell you over the phone."

Penny rested her head in the palm of her hand, her elbow propped up on the desk.

"What have you done?" she asked, quietly.

"You'll see. It'll all make sense in time."

Penny remained silent. She didn't know what to say. Which made it easier for Jock to get the words out.

"Penny-" he added, "thank you for being such an amazing person and my rock. When I hated on the world and didn't trust anyone, you were always there for me. I'm sorry I couldn't give you more of me. I just don't' think I'm that person anymore. My life will always be my job. No matter where I go or what I do."

Penny shook her head. "I love you John," she replied. "You look after yourself."

On those last words, Jock hung up.

Penny sat back in her chair, completely overwhelmed by the phone call and curious as to what was going to be on this USB.

She glanced back up at the computer screen, watching the cursor flash on the last line she'd written.

Jock had left her. She felt emptiness in the pit of her stomach, almost a sensation of nausea.

She wandered what he'd gone and done.

Time would soon tell.

Two weeks later.

Jock opened his eyes. The sun had broken through the hotel window, lighting up the bed. Piercing through his eye lids.

He'd slept in. It was nearly nine o'clock. It was a nice feeling, having nowhere to be.

He flipped back the sheets and sat on the side of the bed, allowing himself to rebalance. He felt spoilt, being able to sleep uninterrupted, without a worry about work, about the women in his life and about what the day would bring. It made him smile.

Jock planted his feet firmly on the floor. The hotel carpet had a much better feel under his feet than the cold floorboards of his bedroom. He'd been toying with the idea of buying a rug, for his room, just never got around to it. Didn't really matter now.

Getting up from the bed, Jock wandered to the bathroom, splashing some cold water on his face as he did every day. He dabbed at his face with the nearby face towel, rubbing his feet into the carpet as he opened the door to his room, picking up the newspaper from the floor and snapping off the rubber band that kept it neatly folded into three.

The headline bought a smile to his face.

'Police Minister implicated in drug and human trafficking ring.'

Reading on, his grin widened, noticing the author of the article. Penelope Acres.

He jumped back into the bed, bringing his knees up, he rested the newspaper on his lap, reading on.

'Members of the Special Operations Group arrested Nikola Petrovic, 48, at a hotel in inner Melbourne at about 1pm yesterday. He surrendered without a struggle, along with his associates at the property.

Members of a newly formed taskforce, codenamed Volcano and led by Detective Inspector Pauline Evans and Detective Acting Sergeant Henry Cornwell ordered the arrests yesterday, which included the long-time serving police minister, Owen Hansen, who was subsequently remanded in custody for his involvement in the drug kingpin's illegal activities.

Detective Acting Sergeant Cornwell told the court that covert audio recordings of both Petrovic and Hansen indicated their involvement in trafficking cocaine and methylamphetamines across the city, along with allegations of human sex trafficking. Police continued to make arrests into the night, as their very own Crime Command was raided. Disgraced Detective Senior Sergeant Shane Johnson was taken into custody with investigators alleging that the senior police boss leaked secret operation details to the drug syndicate and Police Minister.

Investigations are continuing and Detective Inspector Evans indicated more arrests were likely to be made in the coming days as Taskforce Volcano continued to clean up what was left of the infamous Serbian drug cartel.

The Victorian Premier was unavailable for comment last night, however, sources within to the political party indicated it was in damage control, with the arrest of Hansen being the largest criminal scandal to hit local politics in recent memory.

All of those arrested have been remanded in custody, pending their committal hearings likely in the new year.

Jock folded the newspaper over. Closing his eyes, he raised his head to the ceiling and took a deep breath.

There was still a long way to go. Deep down he knew the battle and the war he had waged all those years ago and spent all this time trying to fight, had been finally won.

Blair pulled the unmarked police car into it's parking bay. The view of the surf and the water was an unusual sight. One he wasn't used too. He glanced across at Marcus who had thrown his police compendium onto the back seat.

Both men opened their doors and retrieved their coats which were hanging over the seats. The little seaside town of Lorne was quieter in winter, and it was the first time Blair had been down there since he was a small child.

"She's a tad fresh," Marcus muttered, stating the obvious. "Where's a good place to get an afternoon beverage?"

Blair shrugged his shoulders. "No idea," he replied, "I haven't been down here since I was in primary school."

Marcus turned his nose up. "Your old man didn't get out much then eh?"

It was starting to grow old now. All the comments about his father. He wasn't his father and wasn't sure how to get the message across to his new colleagues without sounding angry or abrupt.

"Yeah I get it," he eventually replied. "My old man was no good. Can we find something else to talk about?"

Marcus laughed. "Whoa, touchy. Easy big fella. Just making fun. No need to get your knickers in a knot."

Blair didn't respond, glancing both ways before crossing the main road.

As the two men found a local café and quiet place to have one last coffee before the day came to an end, Blair took it as an opportunity to get something off his chest. Something that wasn't sitting well with him. He wasn't sure if Marcus was the right audience, but he had no one else.

"I know you've got a gripe with Dempsey," Blair began, "but I need to tell you something in confidence without judgment."

"Did he touch you inappropriately?" Marcus asked.

Blair rolled his eyes. "Seriously."

"Okay okay," Marcus responded, raising both hands in the air as a sign of solidarity. "Go ahead. You can tell me."

"The shooting. Silas Crowley."

"What about it?"

"They retrieved a knife at Silas' home. Dempsey said it belonged to Silas and said he came at him with it. Yet I'm ninety-seven percent certain that I saw that same knife in Dempsey's bag a week prior."

Marcus lowered his coffee. His lack of emotion caught

Blair off guard. He was expecting some form of reaction. Something. Anything.

"It wouldn't surprise me," Marcus eventually said. "That's Dempsey."

Blair glared at him. "That's it? That's all you're going to say?"

Marcus frowned. "Well, did you tell Pauline?"

"No."

"Did they ask you to make a statement?"

"No."

"Did you offer?"

"Well, no."

"So then what do you want from me? Unless you're going to tell someone of importance, it's hearsay from me mate. I can run back and tell the superintendent, but guess who they're going to come for? You."

Blair shook his head. He already knew everything Marcus had said. He was hoping to feel better in getting it off his chest. Yet somehow, he felt worse.

"I know I should have," Blair added.

"So why didn't you?"

Blair leaned back in his chair, thinking of his response.

"I don't think it would do anything. If Crowley was responsible, Jock has probably done the world a favour. No court proceedings. No trial. No cost to anyone."

"That's not how this world works," Marcus interjected. "You're starting to sound like him."

Blair smiled. Reflecting on his time with Dempsey. "Maybe he was onto something. Call me crazy, but I actually enjoyed working with him."

Marcus stood up from the table. "I've heard enough of you talking smack, let's go."

Blair stood up, retrieving his coat from the back of the chair and followed Marcus to the door. Before Blair made it into the door way, Marcus stopped. Holding open the door, he stood in the way before turning to Blair.

"My old Sergeant said something to me when I first joined the homicide squad," Marcus said, still holding the door open, "because back then, there were no rules. We just did what we had too to get a conviction. And it tainted a lot of the old boys, including Dempsey."

"What did he say?" Blair asked.

"He said, *'how far can you go down the wrong path before you can't get back on the right one?'*"

Blair noticed Marcus was serious.

"What I'm trying to say mate is that it's fine to bend the rules. We certainly have to do it from time to time. But when you start doing it to justify a means to an end, that's when you know there's no coming back."

CHAPTER 30

One week later.

He parked his white van on Nicholson Street, right alongside the Carlton Gardens. The parking spot was rare, so he knew how lucky he was to snag it. It made him smile. Everything was going so well. It was also the first Sunday in nearly a month where the sun was out. A sunny day on a weekend in winter was always a treat in the city of Melbourne.

He opened the back of the van, retrieving his fold out camping chair and flinging the strap over his shoulder, he made his way into the gardens. To sit in his usual spot. To just sit and watch. As he did most weekends.

The death of Silas Crowley was perfectly crafted. He'd pushed John Dempsey in the right direction and had caused the perfect confrontation. Planting the hair of Jock's daughter in the make-shift basement at Silas' home was the icing on the cake. He was disappointed that Silas had found out it was planted, but nevertheless, no one was any wiser for it. Not even Dempsey.

Silas death and Nikola's arrest were merely bumps in the

road. He could now deal directly with the buyers which had been the goal he'd orchestrated all along. Dempsey leaving his job was the biggest win for him. It meant the fixation on solving the crimes was now left to no one. Things were looking up and all his hard work had paid off. He'd made sure of that.

He removed the chair from its bag and unfolded it, neatly digging the base of the legs into the thick and lush grass below. Peering around him, it was the usual crowd. Families on picnic's, tourists posing for photos and the occasional weirdo. This time it was a gentleman in baggy fluoro pants juggling coke bottles. He grinned. Perfect.

Then he saw her. She was walking through the park with her family, her long blonde hair dangling freely just above her waistline. She was maybe sixteen or seventeen. Innocent looking. Sharing a laugh with her father. He'd only just setup his chair, they'd be something better coming along soon. It was too early to chase the first one he'd see.

He lent back, hands tucked in behind his head, interlocking his fingers. Allowing the sun to beam down on his face as he closed his eyes.

Then came the shuffling of feet on the pavement. Opening his eyes he recognised the jogger. Black spandex-style three quarter length pants and a white t-shirt. She was red faced from running. Sweat beading on her neck.

"Blair," she said, removing her ear pods from her ears, waving her right hand.

It was Katrina.

"Nice day isn't it?" he replied, smiling.

"Beautiful," she replied, returning pleasantries. "See you

on Monday," she called out, putting her ear pods back in and returning onto the track.

'Well that was awkward,' he thought. Rarely did he bump into people he knew.

He'd changed his mind. Perhaps that blonde teenager was the one after all. He stood up, folding up the chair and returned it to its bag. He'd have to get a move on now if he was going to catch up to them and follow them home.

If there's one thing he's father had taught him all those years ago when he did the same thing it was that you always had to be on your toes. You had to be sharp. He smiled at the very thought of it, recalling those memories. All his advice over the years had worked. It had gotten him this far.

He continued to glance in the direction of his colleague, Katrina, as she ran out of sight. Beyond the row of trees, heading toward the city. As he swung the bag containing his fold out chair up and over his shoulder, he smirked and thought to himself….

'Little do you know'.

One year later.

Detective Sergeant Henry Cornwell lent back in his chair within the police force's crime command office, hitting the 'send' button on his email, agreeing to meet with news reporter Penelope Acres in regard to a follow up story one year on from the launch of Operation Volcano.

It wasn't long after the operation that he was promoted within the ranks, and it helped that Nikola Petrovic was found guilty of his crimes and sentenced to forty years in prison. The entire case was boosted by the statement of an unnamed undercover operative. It still made him smile a year later, knowing that justice was served. Sometimes, just sometimes, the good guys got a win.

There'd been something tugging at the back of Henry's mind for months. The internal investigation into Jock's actions that night were still playing out, as was normally the case for internal disciplinary matters. They could take years to complete. Henry had gotten his hands on the CCTV footage from inside Silas Crowley's home. Three cameras. All hidden and setup by Silas in an attempt to bait John Dempsey into doing something stupid.

Henry had been given a copy of the footage by a colleague within the professional standards division. There were hours and hours of footage, as it appeared that Silas had set the hard drive to not record over itself for thirty days.

Henry rubbed at his eyes, as he bought up the media player once more. Any spare time he had, or at times when he felt like he needed a break from typing, he'd play the footage. In the hope of finding something out of the ordinary. Perhaps something implicating Silas to Nikola. A visit. An exchange. Anything. Except, the footage implicated Dempsey. Whilst it did not show the confrontation between them the night of Silas' death, it did show the comings and goings from the property. A camera hidden in the hallway on a mantle, and another two on the outside of the property. One at the rear, one down the side.

Henry looked to the outdoor footage first, clicking the media player to commence at the beginning, then setting the fast forward to times sixteen. The fastest it would go.

For several hours, and days, it showed nothing.

Then, a figure emerged.

Henry quickly hovered his finger over the mouse to pause, then rewind. He played it again. In normal time.

According to the reports, Dempsey had entered Silas' home a couple of weeks prior to the confrontation, alleging he obtained hair from a cellar.

Except, this footage was earlier. And it wasn't Dempsey on camera.

A dark figure. Dressed all in black. The camera was too high up to capture a clear shot of the face.

'How could the internal investigators have missed this?'

That was Henry's first thought. On second thought, they had their man. They had Dempsey.

Henry switched cameras. From outside to the hallway. The only internal camera he had.

He fast forwarded thirty seconds. Then pressed play.

As expected, the figure emerged again. Except this time, they weren't under the cover of darkness, nor was the angle too high. It was in the perfect spot. Head height. Front on.

Henry threw his hands onto his head, intertwining them as he lent back in his chair. He exhaled deeply. A sense of nausea waivered through his stomach. He couldn't believe what he was seeing. He pressed rewind and hit play again. He had to be sure.

The footage didn't lie.

Dressed all in black with a hood over his head, standing directly in front of the camera. Almost as if he was looking straight at it, was Blair.

Blair Chapman.

At the same time.
Outback Western Australia.
80km east of Mount Magnet.

The 4WD made light work of the dusty road. Normally they would be on their motorcycles, except these roads were unforgiving. It was the easiest way to get to the other regional towns without police interference. The local airports were rife with security, so road was the best way to move drugs. It was easy. No one around for miles on end. Nothing but freight trucks and road trains. Hiding drugs in a car wasn't as difficult as people thought.

Simpson sat in the passenger seat, still wearing his patches. The Fallen Disciples were still in their infancy where motorcycle gangs were concerned. But they had enough members to start covering some ground, particularly around rural western Australia where business was booming and there was little competition.

"Where are we meant to meet this guy?" Simpson quizzed his driver.

Gareth glanced back at him. His neck was killing him from all the driving, but he didn't want to complain. Not to their Sergeant of Arms.

"I think the boss said Paynesville. It's the next stop up ahead."

Simpson rolled his eyes. "I don't trust this new guy."

Billy piped up from the backseat. The smallest of the three, Billy was the loudmouth larrikin of the group. Rarely did he fit in, but the others saw him as nothing more than their annoying younger brother. He had their backs and that's all they asked. He was loyal. Trustworthy.

"You never met the bloke!"

"Shut the fuck up!" Simpson squawked. "No one asked you."

As the car rolled into Paynesville, all three of the boys glanced out of their windows. Nothing around but red dirt and the occasional truck. Paynesville housed a small regional air strip. Windsor Station.

As Gareth slowed the car down, they could see a man in the distance. He looked rough, sporting a short beard and wearing dirty denim jeans. He carried a red backpack and nothing else. His brown boots were covered in red dirt.

"This 'im?" Gareth asked.

"I think so," Billy replied from the backseat. Simpson glanced over at both of them. "You know anyone else that's due to meet us in this fucking desert?"

The two men exchanged a glance.

Gareth pulled the car up alongside the latest addition to their team. The man opened the rear passenger door, pulling himself into the car, he lowered his backpack down into the footwell.

"Who the fuck are you?" Simpson asked, as Gareth floored the accelerator, moving the car back onto the main road and out of town.

The man looked across at Billy, then at Gareth before responding.

"Ditch sent me," the man replied. Simpson nodded, acknowledging the name. Ditch was the president of the Fallen Disciples. A respected figure in the bikie world and whatever Ditch wanted is what he got. No questions asked.

"I'm the newest member of your crew," the man continued, "fuck it's hot out there!"

The four of them sat in silence for a moment, before Billy sat upright, putting his hand out.

"Didn't catch your name."

The man glanced back at him, taking up the offer of the handshake.

"Murphy," he smiled, "Mick Murphy."

ACKNOWLEDGEMENTS

I started this manuscript at the end of 2022 and probably had the idea for it even earlier. Whilst the story is fictional, the characters are reminiscent of a past time, way back when I was walking the beat in inner Melbourne. John "Jock" Dempsey is loosely based around two former colleagues. One of which took me under his wing when I first started and taught me the right way and wrong way of doing things. As they always used to say to new recruits that graduated, *"now we can untrain you and show you how things are done in the real world."*

The other worked as a 'UC' (undercover) and ended up being based out of the western suburbs in Melbourne. He's stories kept me on the edge of my seat and made me understand as a probationary constable that there were parts of the world beyond our reach that were dark and disturbing.

Writing a book is not an easy feat. It takes a lot of patience (something I struggle with) and time. I felt like this one took a lot longer than the others, so the fact that I managed to finish it and get it out for everyone to read is a bittersweet feeling and I am very grateful.

The feedback received from readers across varying forums has been humbling. The fact that I have been asked numerous times, *"when is number three coming out,"* is a great feeling. It's just knowing that readers around the world are enjoying reading these stories as much as I enjoy writing them.

To my family, thank you for your support and constant feedback. My wife is my harshest critic and to quote her directly, *'I didn't like this one as much as the others.'*

To all of my friends, particularly Jarrod. He drops everything to tear the book to shreds as both my self-proclaimed editor and critic. You do it in your own time and never leave a stone unturned. Thank you mate (and thank you to Bryce for allowing you the time).

To Stacey at Champagne Books. You are super-efficient and do an amazing job putting the finishing touches on the end product. I certainly think you've found your calling.

To all of my readers out there—both locally and abroad. Thank-you!

Adam.

Printed in Great Britain
by Amazon